Immortal

LOVE STORIES WITH BITE

Immortal

LOVE STORIES WITH BITE

ഇൻരു

EDITED BY

P. C. CAST

with Leah Wilson

BORDERS®
exclusive

www.teenlibris.com

Developed for Borders, Inc., by BenBella Books, Inc.

Send feedback to feedback@benbellabooks.com

Printed in the United States of America
10 9 8 7 6 5 4 3 2 1

Library of Congress Cataloging-in-Publication Data is available for this title.

Proofreading by Yara Abuata and Emily Brown
Cover art by Ralph Voltz
Cover design by Laura Watkins
Text design and composition by PerfecType, Nashville, TN
Printed by Victor Graphics, Inc.

Contents

Free
Claudia Gray / 159

Introduction

P. C. CAST

So . . . just what the hell is it with you teenagers and vampires? Huh? Well, I have my suspicions. As with any mature, reasoning adult over the age of thirty who is also a parent, my natural inclination is to believe their allure has to do with . . . well . . . sex. I mean, come on! I'll admit to reading *Interview with a Vampire* the year it was released. I won't mention that year so as not to frighten you with my advanced age, but I will say I was sixteen the first time I read the book, and I was definitely tantalized and titillated by the overt sexuality of Anne Rice's vamps.

But while I'm taking this trip way back down Memory Lane, I find that I need to admit to more than just my age. If I'm being honest with myself, and with you, I have to add that the allure of the vampire is much more complex than simple lust. The truth is that vampire appeal goes beyond raging hormones and our baser emotions. I devoured Anne Rice's book and then went on to absorb Bram Stoker's *Dracula* and Chelsea Quinn Yarbro's amazing Chronicles of Saint Germain not just because they were sexy—that's way too simplistic a reason. I got hooked on vampires as a teenager because I identified with them.

About now my adult readers are shaking their heads and thinking, *Cast has lost it . . . again.*

It does sound bizarre. How could a teenager in the '70s, or the 2000s for that matter, "identify" with vampires? Okay, stay with me here. When I was a teenager I understood vamps deep in my soul because, at the very core of my hormone-filled being, I believed I was immortal too. Actually, it was such an innate belief, one that went so hand-in-hand with zits and driver's ed, boy angst and prom, that it wasn't until I looked back in retrospect that I realized what really drew me to absorb all the vampire mythos I could get my hands on.

Think about it. The sensuality and allure of vampires must go beyond biting and blood. Come on! Neither of those things is particularly enticing, even when you add a hot, brooding guy or a sexy chick to the mix. But sprinkle in the ability to live practically forever and to be frozen physically in time so that you don't have to age, and you have a whole new thing. Vampires rebel against time, and they win! Teenagers get that. Because isn't rebelling against time, whether "time" is represented by wrinkles or a parent's disciplinary hand or death itself, what being a teenager is all about?

Of course it is. Or at least it mostly is.

Hopefully you're nodding and grinning and thinking, *Cast hasn't lost it. She's old, sure, but she hasn't lost it. Yet.*

Is it any wonder *Buffy* became such a phenomenon? On one hand, she personified the immediacy of being a teenager. Everything was so deliciously now with Buffy and the Scooby gang. For them, every day really might have been the end of the world. On the other hand, Buffy seemed invulnerable, even to herself, even after she'd died—twice! And who did she fall in love with? Vampires, of course. Yes, Buffy had mortal boyfriends, but she struggled with the fact that it never seemed to work with a regular guy her own age (and species). The characters of Angel and Spike were old, and admittedly, monsters, but Buffy identified and fell in love with them instead. Why? (I mean, besides the fact that they were both so *fiiiine*.) As vampires, they symbolized everything that Buffy, as a teenager, believed would always be exclusively hers: immortal youth and the possibility of forever. And it worked! Spike and Angel hooked the audience along with Buffy, and whether we were fifteen or fifty we wanted to be with them too—to share in the allure of attainable immortality and forever love.

It's a theme I play with in my own young adult vampyre series, the House of Night, which I coauthor with my daughter, Kristin. In our books the teenage heroine, Zoey Redbird, is changing lives and worlds—moving from her human existence to enter the world of vampyres, where she will make the Change into an adult vamp, or die. During this Change Zoey struggles to maintain a relationship with her human boyfriend. In that struggle she's really saying that she isn't ready to fully embrace the magic and passion and foreverness vampyres symbolize. At the same time, she's inexorably drawn to the allure of the vampyre, which is best represented in the character of Erik Night, in whom she glimpses the possibility of forever. It's scary for Zoey, but it also attracts her, just as it attracts the books' readers.

I think that's something else about the vampire mythos teenagers can especially identify with—the sense of fear that goes along with the promise of forever. It's much like the bittersweet fear you feel as you contemplate leaving home for the first time. It's something you desire—something you look forward to and dream about—but there's also a frightening sense of take-this-step-and-nothing-will-ever-be-the-same about it. And yet even that fear itself is exciting, compelling. Vampires carry that same sense of excitement about them. Sure, we can all push through our hesitation and reach for immortality, but perhaps only teens are willing to truly embrace it, because you're used to the big question mark that is the future and you still believe forever can be attained—that youth can really conquer death and love can be victorious over age and apathy.

Because that's really the heart of youth, isn't it? It's the magical possibility of forever that opens before all of us as young adults. When you're a teenager you've become old enough to see the promise of adulthood, you can practically touch the allure of freedom and the mystery of imagining what is to come, but you're also still young enough to believe that you can move through that future without changing, without losing yourself and turning into scary cloned versions of your parents.

And that's what the vampires we fall in love with struggle to do too. No matter the mythos, whether we're lost in the world of Lestat, Edward and Bella, Angel and Buffy, or even my fabulous Zoey Redbird, our immortal enchanters all strive to maintain sense of self and find lasting love over the long stretches of their lives. In these struggles they take us with them and, perhaps, the journey is more magically real for those of you who are still young.

Come with me, will you? Let's pass through the realm of immortals again. I was dazzled by the variety and richness of the stories the wonderful authors in this anthology created. It is always a pleasure to visit Rachel Caine's Morganville, and a familiar joy to be seduced by the magic of Tanith Lee's unique voice and vision. I was a proud mom, smiling at Kristin Cast's world in which vampires were created by the ancient Furies, as well as a satisfied reader. The conclusion of Claudia Gray's pre–Civil War story had me cheering. In "Haunted Love" I was pleasantly surprised by Cynthia Leitich Smith's plot twists and turns. Richelle Mead's "Blue Moon" made me breathless, and Nancy Holder's post-apocalyptic vision took me on a wild, scary ride.

I invite you to join me in reading the magic within these pages. We'll be mesmerized by the allure of the vampire together, and by doing so—even if just temporarily—we'll all attain a measure of immortality.

Haunted Love

CYNTHIA LEITICH SMITH

On my way to work, I pass the worn-out white cottage where I lived as a little kid. The windows are boarded up. So is the door. I expect it'll be put up for auction. I expect it'll go cheap. Nobody's moving to Spirit, Texas.

Every year, the high school grads pack up and leave—one or two for college, the rest for jobs in bigger towns. And every other week, a crowd gathers at the funeral parlor to pay their respects to one of the old folks. Death is the most lucrative business in town.

It seems like everyone dies or leaves. But I'm not going anywhere. Spirit is home. It's the little piece of the world that makes sense to me, which, lately, is saying a lot.

"Cody!" calls a bright, female voice from behind me.

I ignore her. I've never been a talkative kind of guy.

"Cody Stryker!" exclaims the teenage daughter of the new mayor—the one who's going to turn the empty storefronts into antique shops and the abandoned houses into bed-and-breakfasts and offer Spirit a future again, or so he says. "Wait," she pleads. "I need to talk to you."

I pause, turn. Did I say nobody moves here? The girl standing in front of me this evening is an exception to that rule. Last fall, Ginny Augustine and her folks arrived in Spirit after the bank foreclosed on their home in The Woodlands.

Typically, you have to live in town for at least a year before running for office, but nobody else wanted the job, so the city council passed a waiver and Mr. Augustine ran unopposed.

My glare falls to Ginny's hand on my sleeve.

She snatches it back. "I don't believe we've met before. I'm—"

"I know who you are." I begin walking again. Glancing at her sideways, I ask, "What do you want?"

I feel a faint flash of guilt when she blinks, startled.

"Well," Ginny begins again, "someone's cranky. Here's the deal: I'm going to handle ticket sales for you. Cool, huh?" When I don't reply, she adds, "You know, at the theater. Movies? Tickets?"

For the first time in more than fifty years, the Old Love Theater will open tonight at 8 P.M. After Uncle Dean's death, I sold off a third of his cattle, his antique gun, and his fishing boat to make the down payment. None of it was worth much, but neither is the Old Love.

It's reassuring to have somewhere to be on a night-to-night basis, though, to have another purpose beyond satisfying my thirst. To have something else to think about besides the night I faced down my uncle for the last time.

I keep going, trying to ignore how Ginny falls in step by my side.

At sixteen, she's girl-next-door pretty, medium height and curvy. Her teeth are even and pearly white. Long, honey-blonde hair frames her friendly face. What with the powder blue baby T that reads *sassy* in rhinestones and her faded denim cutoffs, Ginny looks like she was born and bred in Spirit, like a real small-town girl.

When we reach the theater, she persists in following me around back.

Ginny leans against the door, coy, as I fish my keys out of my jeans pocket.

"Big night," she observes. "You nervous?"

"No," I lie, unlocking the deadbolt. Once inside, I add, "And I'm not hiring."

"Really?" Ginny asks, shoving a sandal-clad foot in the doorway. "You mean you're going to run the projector, pop the corn, restock the concession stand, ring up food and drinks, vacuum the carpet, change the toilet paper, and do . . . whatever managers do—paperwork and bills—all by yourself? Think about it, cowboy. How do you plan to sell tickets and handle concessions at the same time?"

On one hand, I don't want to encourage her. On the other, I don't need any trouble from her leaving pissed off. I don't need trouble—period. I wish she would just take off. "I'm not opening the concession stand."

"Well, there go your profits! You're charging—what?—three bucks a show? I know people around here are cheap, but do you have any idea what, say, electricity alone is going to cost? It's summer. It's Texas. Think: air conditioning."

Honestly, I hadn't considered that. It's not like I have an MBA or anything. I just graduated from high school a couple of weeks ago. I used to mow lawns in the summer, but this will be my first real job off the ranch. I may have been overambitious.

"Plus," Ginny goes on, "insurance, taxes, and you might want to advertise the place as a tourist attraction. The founders of Spirit were key players in the early days of the Republic, and historical tourism is becoming—"

"Enough." She's a politician's daughter, all right. Opening the door wider, knowing I'll regret it, I say, "Come in. We'll talk."

Ginny quiets as I lead her through the service hallway. It *is* hot in here. Muggy.

I wonder what, if anything, she knows about the building's tragic history, its lingering reputation. A teenage girl—Sonia Mitchell—was found dead in a storage closet in 1959. Another girl, Katherine something-or-other—Vogel maybe—went missing for good. She was new in town, like Ginny, and her body was never found. Both girls worked at the theater. And again, like Ginny, both girls were sixteen.

Everyone hereabouts has heard the story. Partiers have busted in over the years, too, and every now and then a whole pack would run out hollering about a ghost.

There's no denying that the theater has an eerie quality to it. Over the past week, I've seen the letter "S" written in the dust and wiped it away again and again. Once or twice, I could've sworn I heard a soft voice coming from somewhere in the building. Enticing, musical, feminine . . . I'm starting to hear it in my dreams.

As Ginny and I enter the lobby, I don't give her the satisfaction of cranking the air conditioner immediately.

Instead, I take in my new business, trying to see it the way tonight's customers will. It's a grand old place with a huge antique crystal chandelier, built when cotton was king. Granted, the gold and crimson wallpaper is faded, and the blood-red carpet is worn. So are the red upholstered seats in the screening room—both on the main floor and up in the balconies. But there's still a romance to the place, a whisper of the past.

Besides, my mom loved it. Every time we passed by, she'd say the Old Love was a ghost of the glory days of Spirit, a reminder of who we'd been and could become again.

"Do you know how to run a register?" I ask Ginny, gesturing.

She's already playing with it. I only have one, set at the ticket counter. It's an older model that I ordered off eBay.

"Hmm," Ginny says, scanning the lobby before brightening. "I know! We can lay out candy and popcorn on the counter, post prices, and provide a box with a slot in it so that people can pay on the honor system. Like at the library for folks with fines on overdue books."

That wouldn't work in most places. In Spirit, it'll do fine.

"There are some boxes in my office," I say, impressed despite myself. After a pause, I add, "Why do you want this job anyway?"

Ginny shrugs. "I could use the money."

That makes two of us. The thing about living forever, I suddenly need a long-term financial plan. And, I realize, so far as Ginny is concerned, there aren't any other jobs within walking distance. I bet she used to have a flashy car. I bet it was repossessed.

I can't help wondering if there's more to her being here than that. Not to be conceited, but I'm fairly good-looking. I've got Mom's blue eyes, and they stand out against my deep brown skin, slick black hair, and the sharp features I inherited from whoever was my dad. I'm wiry but solid enough from working on Uncle Dean's ranch.

Outside Spirit, girls are always flirting, not that I know what to say back.

The locals, on the other hand, they pity me. When my mom died, everyone said what a shame it was for me to be orphaned at only ten. They saw my bruises in the years that followed. And they knew what Uncle Dean was like.

For a long time, I thought sooner or later somebody would report him to social services—a preacher, a teacher, the school nurse—but it never happened.

I guess most folks were as scared of Uncle Dean as I was.

Ginny is looking at me with an oddly knowing smile, and I realize she's waiting for my decision. I can't help thinking she may be useful. I can't help wondering if she has a boyfriend. But spending quality time around that flesh-and-blood girl is intrinsically problematic. The flesh is a problem. The blood is a problem. At any given moment, it's a toss-up which is worse. "Okay," I say. "You're hired."

The chandelier rattles, distracting us both.

"Drafty," Ginny says, glancing around. "But where's it coming from?"

She asks too many questions. "I turned on the air conditioner."

It's a lie.

⋙⋘

After a ridiculous amount of negotiation, I agree to ten cents above minimum wage, send Ginny home to change into a white button-down shirt, black slacks, and black shoes, and tell her to come back in a couple of hours.

Unlocking the door to my cramped office, I'm less than thrilled to realize that I may need to hire a second person. Someone local. Quiet.

Within the next few years, I need to sew up an understanding with the good people of Spirit. They may not know what I am, but they'll figure it out over time. On the off chance that Ginny's daddy's "revitalization" plan works, I'll be here for generations. I need to reassure them that my presence is no more threatening than the fact that Edwina Labarge collects snow globes or that Betty Mueller talks to her dead husband or that Miss Josefina and Miss Abigail have been "roommates" for more than thirty years.

I'll need front people, I realize, so that the customers who drive in from nearby towns don't notice that the "young" owner never seems to age.

Inside the office, I hit the ceiling-fan light, and begin sifting through the old newspapers and boxes, looking for one that will do for the concession stand.

The headline of a yellowed copy of *The Spirit Sentinel* from June 13, 1959, catches my eye. It reads "City Mourns Daughter; New Girl Missing."

I lift it, studying the black and white picture—Sonia's dimple and laughing eyes. I trace the hairline around her lovely face. Sixteen forever.

I never want to be the kind of monster that destroys innocence like that.

Reaching into my small half-fridge, I grab a bottle of blood, pour a quarter of it into a Texas A&M mug, and pop that into the microwave on the shelf.

Seconds later, I close my eyes, savoring the taste, pushing back the disgust.

I've been this way for only a few weeks.

It's funny. I used to roll my eyes at all those media stories about the trouble kids get into on the Internet. How every generation of grown-ups assumes that whatever's new—from flapper dresses to rock-and-roll to the World Wide Web—is automatically a sign of the apocalypse. My theory was that parenthood triggered amnesia followed by paranoia, though I had to admit it would've been nice to have someone who cared.

Not long after Uncle Dean cracked one of my ribs, I heard at school that there was this guy in Athens, Georgia, selling a "power elixir" on the 'net. I figured it was some kind of steroid cocktail. Probably risky, but it's not like my life was all that safe to begin with. Anyway, the guy supposedly supplied a vat of the stuff to the Varsity football team in El Paso that took state last year.

It was so easy. I "borrowed" Uncle Dean's MasterCard and put in my order. The vial arrived overnight in a box packed with dry ice.

I remember thinking as I unscrewed the cap, *What the hell?*

Nothing could've been more appropriate.

Blinking back the memory, I reach for the bottle to pour myself more blood.

Someone has used a finger to write something in the condensation on the glass. It looks like the letter "S." It wasn't there a moment ago. She's getting bolder, making a bigger play for my attention. It's flattering, I admit. "Sonia?"

☙❧

"What do you think?" Ginny asks, straightening the newly poured paper cups on the concession stand counter.

"Not bad." I have to give her credit. In Ginny's make-do theater uniform, complete with ponytail, she looks like the picture of all-American wholesomeness. She also had her mom swing by Wal-Mart (two towns north) and they picked up ice, several two-liter plastic bottles of Coke (diet, regular, Dr Pepper, Sprite), and several discounted packages of candy bars. It's quite the display of enthusiasm, of *spirit*, you might say.

She grins and grabs a black marker to write out prices and instructions for paying on the honor system. Ginny brought the marker and poster board with her too. I set the box from my office on the counter before she got back. It's already been wrapped in bright gold paper, another Wal-Mart purchase.

My gaze lands on the skin over her jugular. Luckily for Ginny, I'm able to buy fresh-shipped "provisions" from the same site that sold me the original dose.

The night I buried my uncle's body behind the barn, I received an e-mail from the vendor, telling me I qualified for "special customer status" and giving me a code to log in for future purchases. What I found was a series of pages within the site that included a long question-and-answer document about our kind, information on how to mix various blood-wine blends, and from there, an online dating service ("Love That Lasts") extended to all registered members at no additional fee. I admit to clicking through it, despite everything amused by the ads for growing your fangs and shrinking your thighs and finding your "eternal consort." I have *no* intention of going there.

I may be an easy mark, helping to finance some other fiend's long-term retirement. But I got what I wanted. Now I can defend myself against anyone.

I just had no idea that the price would be so high.

ℰℭ

Looking out the theater window onto Main Street, I'm pleased to see a line has already formed—a handful of teenagers and a county deputy with his wife.

This week, I'm showing *Phantom of the Opera*. I've scheduled *The Haunting* with Vincent Price, *Ghostbusters*, and *Ghost* for the three weeks after that.

I'm taking advantage of the place's spooky rep. I hope Sonia doesn't mind. More and more, whenever I fix a loose board or vacuum the carpet or add Crème Caramel potpourri to the ladies' room, I can't help wondering if Sonia approves. I can't help feeling like I'm trying to impress her.

School has been out for a couple of weeks now. The newness of summer has already worn off. Football players and cheerleaders are in double practices, but they're done by sundown and eager to blow off steam. I should be able to pack in the locals and folks from nearby towns, if only because there's nothing better to do.

"Three minutes," I announce, noticing that the line outside is longer now. Much of it is curiosity, I'm sure. But I can build on that.

"That long?" Ginny exclaims, propping up the sign. "The ice will melt."

"The ice will be all right. You're . . . you're doing fine."

I can stand the sunlight, though it seems to weaken me. Just like Ginny's bright smile. She half skips toward the ticket counter and then, with a "Whoa," goes flailing. Without thinking, I pour on the supernatural speed in time to stop her fall.

Ginny steadies herself with a hand on my shoulder. "Where did *you* come from?"

During life, I didn't have friends my age, not in-person friends anyway, just some people I'd chat with on the Internet. It never occurred to me that I'd feel pulled toward someone now. I know better than to care. I ask anyway. "Are you okay?"

"I guess." She straightens. "I could've sworn I tripped over something."

We both glance down at the smooth red carpet.

❧✺❧

Ginny's doing a bang-up job at the register. She's all "yes'm" and "yes sir" with the grown-ups, amicable with the teens, and a charming reassurance that, despite the "haunted" theater and its murderous history, the ghost-movie theme is tongue-in-cheek. We're all just having fun here.

Meanwhile, I'm serving up another row of Cokes. It's great. With the honor pay system, I don't really have to interact with the costumers.

At least not until the deputy shoves a couple of rolled-up dollars into the box and says, "Young Mr. Stryker, isn't it?"

"Yes, sir." I keep my voice level. I've never been in trouble with the law. In fact, I'm known as decent enough—as someone who's had a hard life, but who's respectable, graduated with honors. "Welcome to the Old Love, deputy."

"How's your uncle doin'?" he asks, grabbing a Coke and a box of Milk Duds and a package of red licorice. "Some boys at Hank's Roadhouse were askin' about him."

I knew that, sooner or later, the questions would come. It hurts to be reminded that Uncle Dean had buddies, that there was a better side to him, one I only glimpsed on the rare holiday or when he'd score a big buck.

I swallow the lump in my throat, make a show of glancing both ways, and meet the deputy's eyes dead on. Lowering my voice, I amp my drawl to match his. "Between you and me?"

The answering nod is sharp.

"I'm thinkin' he finally pissed off the wrong man. High-tailed it to Matamoros before the guy came after him. Didn't even say goodbye."

The deputy takes that in. "Good riddance," he mutters as he starts to walk off. Then after handing the Coke to his wife, he turns back toward me, and adds, "I'm glad to see you makin' something out of yourself. Your mama was a fine woman."

For a while, I pour more drinks and offer a "hey" or "howdy" now and then as customers make their selections and pay. But it's not long before I notice the ruckus at the ticket counter.

"Ben, please," Ginny says, her voice rising, "I've got customers."

Ben Mueller was a year behind me in high school. His older brother plays football for Baylor, his mom teaches at the elementary school, and his dad owns a used car dealership on the highway. His granddaddy, Derek Mueller, died two years ago of a heart attack after serving as sheriff for four decades. Ben himself is popular, a solid all-around athlete, and church-going. I only know him by reputation, but he smirks a lot and looks like one of those fungible blond guys on the CW.

"Problem, Ginny?" I ask, approaching.

Ben laughs, and the sound is angry, bitter. "Are you a freak too?"

Behind him, Tricia, the lady who owns the beauty shop, is whispering with her best friend, Martie. They're the unofficial news hotline. If the Old Love becomes known as a place for "wild young hooligans," it's all over. I've got to deal with this fast and without making a bigger scene.

"Ben, please," Ginny says again. "You have to pay or leave."

"Fine," Ben replies. "But just know that I'm—"

I grab his arm, and I can tell he's surprised by the strength of my grip. I stare him in the eye, realizing I'm a couple of inches taller. According to the FAQ on my blood dealer's site, some of us have the power to enthrall the traumatized or weak-willed. It's worth a try. Keeping my voice steady, I say, "You're going to take off now."

"I'm going to take off now," Ben repeats and pivots on his boot heel to stroll out the front door.

I'm surprised that it worked. Again, I don't know Ben well, but I'd never tag him as weak, and as for trauma, anyone could tell he's led a charmed life.

"My hero!" Ginny exclaims, and there's real appreciation in her voice. Then she beams at the two ladies next in line. "May I help y'all?"

ఐలఒ

After the last customer settles in, I get *Phantom of the Opera* running from up in the projector room. Then I hear Ginny call my name. She sounds shocked, terrified.

I half fly downstairs and burst through the swinging door into the ladies' room where she's pointing at *GET OUT*, written on the mirror in plum-colored lipstick.

It wasn't there before we opened. I didn't notice anyone walking into the room before the movie started. From the look on her face, I'm pretty sure Ginny didn't do it, but the color of the lettering matches her lips. She grabs the tube from the counter.

"It's mine," she confirms. "It was in my purse."

I'd stashed the purse in my office for her when Ginny returned this evening.

It must have been Sonia. I didn't know she could do that, move objects. In any case, it's starting to look like she wants to keep the place to herself. I don't understand. We're still getting to know each other, but it was going so well.

"A dumb joke," I say to reassure Ginny. "Let's get it cleaned up."

Ginny opens the small storage cabinet to grab a spray bottle of glass cleaner and a roll of paper towels. "What did you do to Ben?" she asks in a measured voice, and I realize how sloppy I've been.

If I want to stay above suspicion, I'm going to have to learn to deal with people—especially run-of-the-mill troublemakers—without using my powers. No more enthralling. For that matter, no more super speed.

I answer the question with a question. "What's going on between *you* and Ben?"

Ginny begins spraying the glass. "Can I trust you?"

It's a bigger question than she realizes. I'm not sure I know the answer. "You can talk to me," I say. "Ask anyone. I'm no gossip." That's true enough.

She goes to peek out the bathroom door to ensure no one is listening. "Well—"

"Wait. Let's go to my office. It has a lock on it. No one can just walk in."

"But what about . . . ?" she gestures to the mirror.

I shrug. "We'll say it was the ghost."

"Ghost?" Ginny asks.

On our way, I fill her in on the history, characterizing the haunting as local folklore. From Ginny's severe expression, I figure she either finds the idea of ghosts offensive or blasphemous or, at the moment, she's invested in a more corporeal issue.

I let us in, take the desk chair, and wait, trying not to let my impatience show. We can't stay in here long with the door closed. She's still a minor after all.

There's something about her, though, some strange connection between us. I've said more words to Ginny today than I probably have to anyone in the last year.

Ginny crosses her arms. "I don't know the people of Spirit that well yet, nowhere nearly as well as they know each other. I didn't know about Ben."

I lean forward to clear newspapers off a crate for her to sit on. "What about him?"

She takes a seat. "I . . . We went to prom together. Ben got a motel room on the highway afterward. I thought it meant one thing. He thought it meant, um—"

"I understand," I say. A lot of guys have expectations about prom. I can't help wondering how badly Ben took "no" for an answer. The fact that he was still hassling Ginny tonight suggests it was an ugly scene.

"I had to crawl out the bathroom window," she adds.

It could've been worse. "You want me to walk you home tonight?"

"Yes," Ginny pauses, standing again. "No. I'm fine. It's just . . . I never meant for things to turn out this way. I never thought going on one lousy date would—"

"Haunt you forever?" I ask.

She visibly shivers. "How did you know?"

My uncle's face flits across my memory. "Call it a hunch."

§⊃◌℞

Once the last happy customer leaves, Ginny skips across the lobby with a large black trash bag. "Let's get this over with and go celebrate!" With that, she flashes that sunshine grin and disappears into the screening room.

Celebrate? I'm going to have to sit her down and explain that we're employee and employer, that we can't ever be anything more. Except . . . she could use a friend right now. "Hang on," I say. "Let me help you."

I grab a bag, and then it dawns on me that I should probably hit the restrooms first. So, I head down the hall, my steps slowing when I hear the mysterious voice again. "Sonia?" Is that *her* singing? "Sonia!"

I let the plastic bag slip from my fingers onto the red carpet and begin walking faster in the direction of the sound. It's louder, clearer with each step I take.

I've heard the song before. Spirit only gets three radio stations— one in Spanish, one that plays country western, and one that plays golden oldies. It's a 1950s hit, "To Know Him Is to Love Him." It's kind of sweet and kind of insipid and, once you've heard it, it's hard to get out of your head for the rest of the night.

The voice leads me to the door of a dingy break room that, in the push toward the grand re-opening, I decided to worry about later. I'm reaching for my keys when the supposedly locked door opens on its own.

Inside, the temperature is cooler, much cooler than it should be, especially with the vents shut. I'm greeted by the sight of a sink and cabinets, an empty space where a full-size refrigerator used to be, a beat-up table big enough for six, and five metal chairs.

The voice is coming from one of ten rusty half-lockers lined against a wall.

I'd hold my breath, but breathing is optional. "What are you trying to tell me?"

When I open the locker, it's empty. The voice grows louder, the room colder.

From behind, I hear something smack the table. Turning fast, I see the dust still flying up from where the little cloth-bound book landed. I walk over, and the song dissipates with each step I take, ending altogether when I pick up the . . . it's a diary.

I flip through the entries, each signed with the letter "S." I slip out an old photo of a lovely dark-haired girl, the same girl whose photo is on the front page of the 1959 copy of *The Spirit Sentinel* in my office. She's cuddling a tabby kitten.

Amazing. After a lifetime as a loner, I suddenly have two new girls in my life.

Ginny is easy enough to figure out. But Sonia? The singing, the diary, even the mysterious "S" here and there all seem a lot more welcoming than the *GET OUT* in the bathroom. Does she really want me to leave, or is she just playing along with the haunted-theater theme?

A moment later, from across the building, Ginny cries out again.

When I reach the screening room, she's clutching her right forearm. Blood is dripping through her fingers. I can smell it. I can almost taste it. I feel my fangs slide.

I pause to regain control, calling, "Ginny!" like I can't spot her toward the front, bent in the aisle.

"Over here," she says, straightening, her face covered by her honey-colored hair.

I jog to her side. "What happened? Did you cut yourself on a chair?" They're old, and the heavy cushioned seats fold down. She could've torn her skin on a spring.

"No." Ginny lifts her hand from her arm to show me three short, deep scratches. They look like fingernail marks. Sounding mystified, she adds, "It was like being clawed by the wind."

Sonia. I catch myself licking my lips. "You need stitches. Let's—"

"No," Ginny replies. "It's fine. I was just surprised."

"It'll scar," I insist.

"Give me your shirt," she counters.

"Wha—"

"Your shirt. So I can use it to, you know, apply direct pressure."

Embarrassed by the misunderstanding, I'm already unbuttoning by the time she's finished the sentence. I fold the material as best I can and tie it around her arm.

"My hero," Ginny says again. She rises on her toes to kiss my cheek and, losing her balance, her lips land, lingering, on my throat instead. "About that celebration . . ."

"Go home, Ginny," I say, moving away.

She looks stricken, like the child she is. "But . . ."

I lighten my tone. "I mean, you'd best be getting home."

I watch her walk up the aisle, fuming, and disappear out the door.

Then a disembodied voice—soft, musical, and furious—whispers in my ear, "Murderer, murderer, murderer."

❧◌◖

Later, at my uncle's ranch, I walk to his unmarked grave behind the barn. I buried him deep, wrapped in a Mexican blanket. The ground is bare, packed hard. I try to tell myself it's more fitting that he's here instead of at the old cemetery in town. Uncle Dean loved this land as much as he was capable of loving anything.

The grave unsettles me, though. No stone, no cross. He may not have been a good man, but he was my mom's big brother.

As dawn approaches, I shake off the guilt and go inside.

Now, I'm surfing the Web at the dining-room table, drinking microwave-heated blood and researching ghosts. Sonia's history does track with what I've learned so far. Her death was traumatic. Her murderer was never caught. In the spirit world, that's textbook "unfinished business." A reason to haunt. And it's clear that Sonia wants me to know who she is—writing her initial and giving me the diary are clear enough hints.

According to the newspaper article, though, Sonia was a sweetheart. She used to teach Sunday school and run errands for her elderly neighbors. A quick skim of the diary—peppered with initials—confirms that she was a good-hearted girl with loopy handwriting and typical teen angst: homework, a boy ("D"), a rival girl ("K"). She adored Elvis ("E"), had a kitten named Peso ("P"), and collected toys at Christmas for the poor.

Maybe Sonia thinks I'm a threat to Ginny, and she wants me to know she's on to me. I'm not sure why she attacked Ginny, though. Maybe in her ghostly state, Sonia's confused. Or maybe she's trying to protect Ginny by scaring her off.

I guess there's always the possibility that the Old Love is home to more than one ghost. Katherine, the girl who went missing, is probably K. According to the diary, she and Sonia didn't get along in life. But there's no hard evidence of more than one entity, and the singing voice that lead me to Sonia's diary in the break room matched the accusing one that whispered "murderer."

Besides, how many dead people could possibly be hanging around the place?

In any case, I can't overlook the lipstick message or the fact that Ginny was injured. If I can't somehow convince Sonia (or whomever) that I'm not dangerous, I'll need to force her out. Either that or my effort to resurrect the Old Love is over.

The question is, how? I'm in no position to be calling a minister or priest.

Worse, the ghost who spoke is right. I can be lethal. I have killed once before.

I take another swig of blood and notice that my caller ID is blinking. Ben Mueller. He didn't leave a message.

Why would Ben call here? Does he seriously think Ginny came home with me last night? It's not like I've got any kind of rep with girls. Then again, he knows Ginny better than I do, and considering the way she kissed my neck. . . .

Still, calling after the way they fought earlier, that's stalker behavior. Maybe Sonia's right to fret Ginny's safety, only she's worried about the wrong guy.

℁⊙⟫

The following evening, patrolling the theater hallway, I don't hear any singing. I don't step into a cold spot. I don't see a fresh letter "S" written anywhere.

Today I was the one who fetched refreshments. I also made some calls, ordered a regular shipment of candy, popcorn, and Coke. Tonight I have to put Sonia to rest.

Ginny comes bounding into the lobby at 7 P.M. sharp. She's wearing a different white shirt, its sleeves down and buttoned at the wrists.

"How's your arm?" I ask from the concession stand.

Ginny shrugs. "It looked worse than it was."

"And Ben?" I press. "Has he bothered you again?"

She glances at the front doors. "Not today."

It's then that I hear Sonia whisper "murderer" in my ear again.

"No!" I exclaim. At Ginny's expression, I add, "Not you." I run a hand through my hair, frustrated. "I'm sorry, but you're going to have to leave. We're not opening tonight. There's . . . Someone's here. This is going to sound crazy, but she's a—"

"Ghost?" Ginny raises her scratched arm. "Yeah, I already figured out that much. And personally, I say we exorcise the bitch."

Wow. That was the last reaction I would've expected. I can't help admiring Ginny's bravery, though. Maybe we could have a future after all, if we're willing to fight for it.

I glance at my mom's Bible, wrapped in a kitchen towel, on the concession counter. I don't know whether I'll burst into flames if I touch it. I don't know what I'm doing at all. Even though Sonia lashed out at Ginny, I can't help having mixed feelings about taking her on. After all, I'm no innocent, and by all accounts, she used to be.

"Seriously, let's do it now." Ginny takes a step in my direction, only to be violently shoved back by a whirlwind, a fierce wall of air, separating us.

Candy and cups fly off the counter, splattering Coke. A bloody slash appears on Ginny's forehead. The crystal chandelier shakes and sways.

"Sonia!" I shout, trying to reach Ginny. "Sonia, please! Listen to me! You're making a mistake! Don't you see? You're hurting her!"

"Murderer!" returns Sonia's voice, this time louder than mine. "Murderer!"

"I—" Do I have to admit it? Is *that* what it'll take? "I'm . . ."

Ginny is knocked onto her back. She struggles like she's being choked by invisible hands. She kicks with both legs. Then she's lifted, spun, and dropped again.

I reach back for the Bible, letting go as pain flashes across my fingertips.

I don't understand. Sonia knows that *I'm* the monster. Why target Ginny, not me?

For a split second, I wonder if Sonia is jealous, if the girls are fighting over me. But then Sonia wails "murderer, murderer!" again.

"You're right! Sonia, you're right!" I never intended to kill my uncle, even though sooner or later, he probably would've killed me. I just wanted to become stronger, strong enough to protect myself. I didn't know that the blood lust would come with that strength. I hadn't gained control of it yet. "Sonia, stop! Please! Punish me!"

I'm resigned to face her judgment when Ben tears into the lobby from the service hallway. He has a battle-axe in one hand and—dear

God—the decapitated heads of Ginny's parents, by the hair, in the other.

Ben tosses them onto the red carpet. "Howdy, Ginny!"

Has Sonia possessed him? Has he lost his mind?

Ginny is on her knees, her head bent, her hands covering her face. She's an easy target.

"Murderer, murderer, murderer!" Sonia charges again.

Ben hesitates, his gaze searching for the speaker.

"Sonia!" I duck a box of Milk Duds that whizzes by. I want to help. I need to, but the supernatural wind is holding me back. "Let her go! He'll *kill* her!"

Ginny looks so small, huddled on the red carpet. We've known each other only a couple of days, but she's brought sunshine into my life and made me feel like I belong in the glow. It's not love. It's the hope of love. But it's the closest I've come to it since I was ten years old. If Ginny wants me, how can I be a monster?

I reach for the Bible again and hold it over my head, ignoring the pain. "In the name of . . ." I raise my voice, start again. "In the name of the Father, the Son—"

With a roar, Ginny raises her face. Her mask of innocence melts away, and I see her for what she is. Undead. Demonic. Like me, a vampire.

I drop the Bible, clenching my blistered hands. "Ginny?"

Ben looks from her to me, like he's trying to figure out whose side I'm on.

"I was going to tell you," Ginny says, her voice pleading. "When your profile showed up on the system, I thought it was a sign." Her shoulder jerks, struck by the ghost. "I want the kind of love that lasts."

The system. "Love That Lasts." She's talking about the blood dealer's matchmaking service. Ginny must have the same supplier.

"Sonia!" she screams. "Don't you have anything better to do? You were a loser in life, and you're still a loser now. I told you this town would be mine someday!"

"Murderer!" Sonia replies. "Katie, murderer!"

So, Ginny was the one who killed Sonia. Sonia was never trying to scare her off, to protect her from me. When Sonia said "murderer," I wasn't the one she was talking about. Ginny had been Katie, Katherine, the girl whose body was never found.

From her crouched position, Ginny lunges at Ben as a swath of blood appears across her torso, staining the white shirt. She knocks the axe from his hand and kicks his boots out from under him. He's no match for her.

Ginny can't fight Sonia, but she could tear Ben apart.

"Let me help him," I say, and the ghostly force dies as quickly as it rose. I vault over the concession stand, snatch the axe from the carpet, and stand between them.

For a moment, I see the hope in Ginny's eyes. Unlike Ben, she knows that I'm one of her kind. She's already admitted that she wants me. She's already called me her "hero" twice. I slowly shake my head, leaving no doubt about my intentions.

"You wouldn't," Ginny breathes as reality sinks in. She's been beaten by me, Sonia, and Ben together. Her voice is resigned. Her last words are: "Daddy had such big plans."

I sever her head with the blade and, shaking, drop the axe handle.

After a stunned moment, Ben climbs to his feet and puts a hand on my shoulder. "You okay, man?"

"Better now," I say. "You?"

"She came after me on prom night," he explains. "I've been trying to run her out of our town ever since."

Our town. Ben is Spirit. I'm Spirit. God knows Sonia is Spirit.

Ginny was the new girl again, this time with a new name.

"I tried to warn her off," Ben adds. "I tried to scare her off. I went to my family for help, but nobody believed me. She didn't seem like a vampire, you know?"

"Yeah, I know."

What happened here will stay with Ben for a long time. He isn't the kind of person who can destroy someone else, even something else, without it weighing on him. I know how he feels and then some.

ℰℭ

It's been two weeks since that night, since the last time I noticed any sign of Sonia. I already miss her. I'm sorry for having doubted her goodness, and I'm glad that the monster who killed her will never hurt anyone again.

Ben and I burned Ginny's and her parents' bodies (heads too) behind my barn. We buried the axe, which he'd taken from the mayor's office, near my uncle.

"Come spring, you might sprinkle some wildflower seed on the graves," he said. "I mean, they were human beings once."

I said I would and made a mental note to sprinkle seeds on Uncle Dean's grave too.

The next day Ben fibbed to his aunt Betty that the Augustines had packed up and left in the middle of the night for some six-figure job that the mayor landed up north. Ben explained that Ginny told him her dad was too embarrassed to own up to running out on the town after all his big promises. He claimed that's what their spat in the ticket line had been about.

Betty repeated the story the next day at the beauty shop, and it's become common knowledge since. The deputy is circulating a petition to put his own name on a mayoral ballot. I signed it last week.

Turns out, Ben's not a bad guy. His granddad, Sheriff Derek Mueller, had been the vampire hunter who originally chased the Augustines out of town back in the day. The sheriff had passed on what he'd seen, what he'd learned, to Ben so Ben would know what to do if the homicidal undead ever swung back through town.

Ben has decided to work at the Old Love and save up for college. Apparently, being a good athlete by Spirit standards isn't necessarily the same as being scholarship material. Facing down the undead has grown him up a lot.

He doesn't know what I am, not yet, but he took it well when I explained about Sonia. I hope that when the day comes, when he realizes I'm not just another home-town boy, he thinks back on what happened and gives me the benefit of the doubt.

Tonight after the Ghostbusters save New York City, I thank Ben for a good night's work, lock the front door behind him, and once again hear Sonia singing "To Know Him Is to Love Him."

When I look toward the voice, I see Sonia herself for the first time. She's taken over one of my jobs, wiping down the concession counter, like it's no big deal.

Sonia is a see-through figure in a uniform not much different than the one Ginny wore, except that Sonia's includes a red vest with a gold patch that reads "Love Theater."

I didn't realize she was still here. I don't get it. With Ginny gone for good, why stick around? "Sonia?"

She raises her face, and I see the dimple, the laughing eyes. "Cody!"

"Sonia," I say in case she didn't understand what happened, "your murderer has been destroyed. It's over. You can move on now. You can, uh, go into the light."

Sonia tilts her head. "It wasn't all about justice." Her voice has a hollow quality to it. "Tell me, Cody. Do you believe in love at first sight?"

Staring at her, God help me, I just might. I read on the Web that the more you believe in a ghost, the stronger your feelings for them, the more substantial they become.

With each passing second, Sonia appears more solid, more alive. And I have to admit, in some ways, we would be perfect for each other. We're both tied to this old theater, we'll both be teenagers forever, and we're both dead. Even better, I don't have to worry about physically hurting her. No flesh. No blood. No problem.

This could become more than the hope of love. It could become the real thing. But there's something she has to be told first. She may not know what happened at my uncle's ranch, but I thought she'd figured out what I am from the bottle of blood in the office mini-fridge. I guess Sonia didn't realize what the liquid was or maybe in her ghostly state, some details are fuzzy.

"Sonia," I begin again as she floats toward me. "There's something you should know. I'm a monster, the same kind of monster—"

Her cool fingertips press against my lips, and in her gaze, I see complete understanding, total acceptance. "No," Sonia says. "You're not."

Amber Smoke

KRISTIN CAST

*F*rom their place in the bowels of the Underworld, the Furies, Daughters of Night, summon their son. They are skeletal winged creatures, the black of rotting flesh thinly stretched across their hunched, quivering bodies, not much more than flesh sacks barely able to contain the power of each of their morbid talents.

"Alekossss, come."

He was birthed eons ago from the womb of vengeance, conceived by jealousy, and grown in constant anger. Bred to defend mortals, he was sent from their underground realm to the world above, and there, away from their poison, he learned compassion. At first only so that he could mimic and blend. Later, after centuries, humanity took hold within him, causing the Furies unending confusion with their errant son, this man who grew up and away from them.

Alekos appears, his Herculean body glowing from the descent, the return home. "Yes, my mothers?" He steps down from the ledge he was summoned to, his torn jeans dragging through the souls of the doomed as he strolls toward the three creatures in the dark. He can hear their wings rustling with the excitement of his return. Although he had been there only weeks before, they had not seen him in years. Time ticks by slowly below. As he approaches, they gently grab him and lead him farther into the nothing, farther from the whines of the tortured.

"Ssssit." They command. He sits and puts his feet nonchalantly up on the table.

"The longer you're up there, the more disgusting and human you become." Their throats click and rattle as they speak as one.

He removes his feet and snaps his fingers. Oil lamps flicker on, revealing a cave wet and putrid with chaos and death. The three figures huddle together staring at their son across a crude stone table on which sits a bouquet of night-blooming moon flowers the delicate color of infants' flesh. Slowly they begin to rock back and forth as if they are one and not three. Their eyes are dark and endless, and drip with the blood of the tortured. The snakes in their hair alternate between attacking and caressing one another.

"The Fates have decided. Her cord isss being cut tonight." At first they speak as one, then break apart, finishing each other's thoughts.

"You mussst find her,"

"give her life,"

"sssssave her,"

"sso ssshe can"

"give usss"

"vengeance."

The Furies click with amusement as his mind is flooded with pictures of a beautiful young woman: long chestnut hair, chocolate eyes, olive skin, and a black dress. They have chosen her for him. He blinks and stands. Alekos knows he was only there for this—the gift of his mission. It is now time for him to depart, and for the first time in centuries he feels nervous, excited, alive.

"Thank you, mothers." He turns to leave. "Oh! Furies, mothers." He glances back to see them still swaying. "Where do I find her?"

They close the black holes that served as their eyes, grip each other tightly, and send their too beautiful son to the modern world with the sounds of their shrieks echoing their farewells.

☙☙

Stop and stare. You start to wonder why you're here not there.

Ryan Tedder's melodic voice came booming out of my black cell phone, waking me from a much-needed nap. I groped around my nightstand unsuccessfully for my glasses. Seriously blind as a bat, I quickly gave up on reading the glowing caller ID box. Instead I flipped open the phone.

"Hello?"

"Oh my God, Jenna. Were you sleeping?" The annoyed tone picked me up out of the dream world I was loitering in and threw me back into reality.

"Bridget? No! Sleeping, me? No!" I perkily pretended.

"Good! Well, I was just calling to remind you to bring your camera tonight. We're going to have so much fun at Taylor's hotel party! I can't wait! Being seniors is sooo much fun! What are you wearing?"

"Umm, I think my little black strapless dress with my mom's new gold shoes."

Bridget sucked in air. "No way! Those new strappy heels from Saks? That is so not fair! We're going to look super hott, like always. Ugh, hang on, my mom is yelling at me." She moved the mouth piece of her cell away and I could hear her muffled whines at her mom. "*Okay, Mom.* She wants me to tell you not to forget your cell phone because that gross serial killer guy just killed someone else. Well duh, he's a *serial* killer, jeez. Sorry, she is so protective and weird. But anyway, I have to go finish getting gorgeous. See you at the Ambassador at ten! Love you, and don't forget the digital!"

The line went dead. *How is she always so happy?*

I stood up, stretched, found my glasses laying on the floor next to my nightstand, and looked at the clock: 7:57 P.M. *Crap. No time for a shower.*

As I sleepily wandered the five feet from my bed to my ocean-themed bathroom, I could hear my mom screeching at me from her room down the hall. "Jenna! Do you know where my gold strappy shoes are? I just bought them and they've already *mysteriously* disappeared." She walked into my room and looked around.

I poked my head out of the bathroom door, my hair falling straight into the toothpaste I had just squeezed onto the brush. "Mom! If you're going to come in here anyway, *why* do you have to yell at me from down the hall?"

"Saves time. Which I don't have much of. Paul's going to be here," she looked down at her watch, "in less than an hour. So?"

"Oh, umm, nope. Haven't seen 'em. Sorry." I hardly ever lie to my mom, she's too good at catching me, but this was different. It was the first party of my senior year of high school, and I had to look the best. And I'm sure Paul had seen them already. She's been with the nerdy mortician for like six months. Besides, gold is hot right now, ask anyone.

"Hmm, well, if you see them let me know." She wasn't looking at me; instead, she continued to take inventory of my room.

"Yeah. Okay." I sighed trying to keep the annoyed *I'm running late too* tone out of my voice. I stuck the toothbrush into my mouth.

She started to leave, and her dark curls bounced around her shoulders, making her suddenly look a lot younger than a forty-something-year-old mom. She paused at the door. "And Jenn, don't forget to take Mr. Pepper. He's in his spot by the front door."

Oh Lord, Mr. Pepper. Ugh. I want to actually be popular this year, not be known as "the girl who carries around pepper spray."

I finished brushing my teeth, put my contacts in, and stood staring in the mirror at my messed-up locks. "Up-do!" I decided.

I began wrapping my fingers around my tangled hair in an attempt to turn it into an intentionally messy low pony when the cute Ryan Tedder again blared through the room. I quickly clipped up my hair and glanced down at the sink where I had set my phone. "Connor!" The picture of his goofy smile, sandy shaggy hair, and gray eyes made my stomach jump.

"Hey." I answered casually, pretending not to be excited.

"Hey. I thought you'd never answer. What are you doin'?"

"Nothin'." I rolled my eyes. *Nothin'? I am so lame.*

"Oh, well, that's cool. I just wanted to see if you're coming to Taylor's thing tonight. There's gonna be a DJ, and his older brother's bringing vodka and beer and stuff, so it should be pretty awesome."

Of course I'm going. It's only like the biggest social event of the semester! "Umm, yeah. I think Bridge and I'll probably make an appearance."

"Good. I'll definitely look for you then."

"Definitely. See ya tonight." I hung up before I could start rambling about my undying love for him. *Oh my God he's so f-ing hot!*

I fought off the urge to call Bridget and babble semi-hysterically about Connor actually calling me, and instead trotted to my closet on a wave of happy he's-almost-my-boyfriend thoughts, where my black Tinkerbell cocktail dress hung waiting. Then I began digging my mom's cute gold shoes out of hiding from under my dirty clothes.

Sadly, Mom chose that instant to prove her radar wasn't fading with age. Thankfully, she knocked on my open door, giving me a split-second of warning.

I jumped. "Mother!" I tried to plaster on an innocent smile as I jerked around to look at her.

"I'm not yelling this time. Ew." She looked at the wad of clothes I'd grabbed to camouflage her shoes. "Don't tell me you're wearing something dirty to your little get-together thing tonight."

"No, Mom, I'm just looking for my, uh, headband. You almost made me pee on myself."

"Sorry. Anyway, Paul's here so I'm heading out on my *date.* Maybe I'll even have a little sex. Hehe." She made herself giggle and turn red as she left me with that disgusting mental picture.

Oh barf! Is everyone having sex except me? I stood up and thought about Connor. *Wait! It's been an hour already?!* I whipped around to face the clock: 9:03. *Shit.* I frantically dressed myself, found the shoes, and ran into the bathroom to put on my face. Luckily, it only takes a little eyeliner and mascara to bring me back from the dead. I checked my phone: 9:21 P.M. *Okay, shoes, and then the thirty-minute drive to the Ambassador.* The shoes, however gorgeous they may be, took about twenty minutes for me to buckle. I'm not a contortionist; feet aren't supposed to bend like that. Stupid (gorgeous) shoes.

I ran downstairs, grabbed Mr. Pepper and my gold clutch, checked for lip gloss and my ID, and nearly tore the key hook out of the wall in my efforts to bolt out the front door.

"Please start." I sent out a quiet prayer as I ran down the front sidewalk, crunching autumn leaves on my way. I got in and turned the key to my 1969 cherry-red Mustang. It's a super cute car, it just doesn't always run.

Vrrrrrooomm. "Success!" I took off down the street and got about five miles away from my house before my super cute car died. I dropped my head against the steering wheel, banged it a few times, and felt around the passenger seat for my cell phone. "Of course, you forgot it, Jenna. And the camera! Dammit! Bridget's gonna be pissed!" I slouched down in my seat, smashing the puffiness of my dress, and silently cried for my mommy.

As if my mom had miraculously appeared, her words trickled in through my tears: "Jenn, use your bus pass, you silly girl. I got it for you because your car kind of sucks." *Well, duh.* I stopped crying and checked my eyes in the rearview mirror. Thank God for waterproof eye makeup and close bus stops. My mom's gold shoes were definitely not made for walking.

When I got to the bus stop I chose to stand alone while three other people crammed themselves on a bench made for two. *This would be so much easier and way less gross if I had just remembered my* phone. *Now I have completely passed being fashionably late and entered the "you think you're too good to actually be here" time. And what if Connor is dancing with someone else?!*

"It's you." A male voice broke through my internal rant. *Great. I haven't been here ten minutes and I'm already getting hit on by a bus person creeper.*

"Well, I'm glad you think so." I crankily angled my back toward him and turned my attention to my clutch and my friend Mr. Pepper. *I have got to get a new car.*

"You don't understand. You're—"

I could feel him getting closer so I shoved my hand into my clutch. "No *bud*, I don't think you understand! If you say another syllable in my general direction," I whipped out the pepper spray so the Mr. Pepper label was clearly visible, "I will spray this right in your—holy hell!"

☙❦ৎ

I sucked in enough air to oxygenate a small country as I shot off of my pillow.

Stop and stare. You start to wonder why you're here not there.

My hands were shaking so badly that I could hardly open the phone. "Hello?"

"Hey Jenna! I was just calling to remind you to bring your camera tonight. We're going to have sooo much fun at Taylor's hotel party! I can't wait! Being seniors is sooo much fun! What are you wearing?"

"My black dress with my mom's new gold shoes?" Huh? What? I rubbed my face, trying to reorient myself.

Bridget gasped. "No way! Those new strappy heels from Saks? That is so not fair! We're going to look super hott, like always."

I interrupted her rambling, "Is this a joke, Bridget?"

"Jenn, you know I take fashion and parties very seriously. Are you okay? You're weren't sleeping, were you?"

"Umm, no, no. I'm fine. Just having a mad case of déjà vu." Thirst burned the back of my throat and my head pounded with confusion. I was *not* okay.

"Creepy. Anyway, try not to go crazy 'til after tonight, k? Ugh, hang on, my mom is yelling at me." Bridget's familiar whines were muffled. "She wants me to tell you not to forget your cell phone because that gross serial killer guy just killed someone else. Well duh, he's a *serial* killer, jeez. Sorry, she is so protective and weird. But anyway, I have to go finish getting gorgeous. See you at the Ambassador at ten! Love you, and don't forget the digital!"

I closed the phone, then dropped it on the floor and fell back onto my fluffy down pillow.

"What in the hell kind of dream was that?" I rolled over and looked at my clock: 7:57 P.M., *weird.*

"Jenna! Do you know where my gold strappy shoes are? I just bought them and they've already *mysteriously* disappeared."

I hesitated, staring at her as she stood in the doorway. She was surrounded by a strange vanilla-colored cloud of mist. I rubbed my eyes and blinked a few times, and it went away. "Mom, what did you say?"

"My shoes. The gold ones. From Saks. Look, Jenna it's okay if you wore them, but I really don't have time for this. Paul's going to be here," she looked down at her watch, "in less than an hour. So?"

"Umm, no, I haven't seen them."

"Hmm, well, if you do let me know." Puzzled, she stared at me with her forehead all scrunched.

"What?"

"Nothing, for a second you just seemed different. Well, have fun tonight. Oh! And Jenn, don't forget to take Mr. Pepper. He's in his spot by the front door."

I sat up in bed, staring out the door. *It was just a dream. A really weird, freaky dream. I bet if I think about it longer I'll have played poker with the beaver and Abe Lincoln like in that insomnia commercial.*

Ow! White light burned through my mind along with a picture and a memory. I had an insanely vivid flash of the guy at the bus stop, and two words screamed through my mind: *"FIND ME!"*

"What the hell!" I lifted up the covers to make sure I was wearing clothes and had all of my limbs. *Completely intact. What is going on?*

I heard from beside me: *You start to wonder why you're here not there.*

Leaning over, I slowly picked up my phone from off the floor. Connor. Just like before. This time I hit the ignore button with shaky fingers and turned the phone on silent. *Maybe I need some water. I'll rehydrate. Wake up.* As I got out of bed, I felt something jab the bottom of my foot. I picked up the frame to my glasses, which I had just smashed. *Wait. I can see? I shouldn't be able to see.* I stuck my finger in my eye. No contacts. *Weird déjà vu dreams curing blind-as-a-bat-ness?*

I stared at myself in the bathroom mirror. *Is this what people look like when they're crazy? What the hell? What the hell? What the hell?* "Jenna, just go get some water and some extra-strength Tylenol," I told myself, hoping speaking my thoughts out loud would bring some sanity to my mind.

As I walked past my mom's open door on my way downstairs to the kitchen I heard her weirdly familiar words.

"Hey! Paul's here so I'm heading out on my *date*. Maybe I'll even have a little sex. Hehe." I cringed as she flitted past me. *That doesn't get any better the second time around.* I glanced at the clock on the wall: 9:03.

I took comfort in doing something as normal as getting a glass from the cabinet. My cabinet, my normal cabinet. And water from my sink, my normal sink. A cool fall wind blew in through the partially open window, bringing the familiar smell of autumn leaves to me. Just like before. Just like when I was walking to my car. My brain launched itself into another flashback seizure as my mind's eye filled with another painful vision. I dropped my glass and it shattered, raining shards of crystal at my feet.

"*FIND ME!*" The voice, *his* voice, sounded more impatient, and it was coupled with images from the bus stop.

Then I knew. I don't know how, and I don't know why, but I knew he was there waiting.

⁝⁞

I didn't even notice anything wrong with my foot until I was upstairs putting on my shoes. I was shocked by the small pieces of glass that had stuck in my heel. Blood was staining my fuzzy green carpet. As I painlessly pulled out the glass, I brought it to my face. Holy crap! My blood wasn't my blood anymore! It was no longer bright red and penny-smelling. Instead it was dull amber, and the sweet, soothing smell relaxed me and made me feel at home.

I really need to find this guy who's in my head.

My foot was completely healed by the time I put on my Coach tennis shoes and ran down the stairs and out the door. *Am I like that chick off of* Heroes? *The one who heals herself over and over again?*

I hesitated as I reached my car. "Jenna, maybe driving is not such a good idea. Not only are you getting weird voicemails in your head, but today seems to be some sort of twisted repeat, so why would your car work this time?" I find that sometimes talking to myself is the best way to sort through my problems, and I am such a good listener. "Where is a do-gooder neighbor when you need one?" I looked but of course, chivalry is dead, and so was my neighborhood.

"Aaaah! I just want to be at the freaking bus stop, people!" I closed my eyes and threw a mini temper tantrum, stomping my foot like a toddler in a toy store. There was a sudden rush through my body that made me feel like I was falling off a tall building. When I unsquished my face and looked around I realized I was there, at the freaking bus stop! And I was sitting on my butt in the middle of the sidewalk.

"Well, that's not right."

"Hey! Hey! Shit!" yelled a familiar male voice.

"You!" I scrambled backward through a pool of my amber blood, and was amazed when I felt only adrenaline and not one bit of pain from coming into such close contact with the concrete. "I've gone completely insane and it's all your fault! Turn me back!" He reached out and grabbed my flailing hands to pull me up and I was smothered by a rush of calming autumn air. My eyes opened super wide and fixed on him.

"You okay?" He cocked his head to the side and stared back.

"I—I think I'm bleeding." Pressing my hand against the back of my head, I came in contact with damp tangled hair. No wound, no pain, just really nappy wet strands. "Well, I thought—"

His smile was slow and a little sarcastic. Actually it was almost a smirk. He shook his head. "What you thought is not even close to the truth."

"Huh?" I said, brilliant. Okay, the guy was so majorly hot it was making it hard for me to think. Tall and blonde and delicious. A complete Justin Hartley look-alike. *Yummmm.*

"Alek." He stepped back just a little and extended his perfect hand. "My name is Alek, and I need you to trust me."

Not knowing what else to do, and feeling completely, utterly overwhelmed, I stuck out my hand for him to shake, and added my best attempt at a hair flip. "I'm Jenna," I said, while the leaves danced around my feet.

"Jenna, you must come with me." He was looking at me with his incredible green eyes.

"Uh, no, I have to—"

He covered my hand with his. He felt warm and strong and the only real thing that had touched me since I'd fallen into this nightmare.

"You have to come with me," he repeated. "Trust me. I'll tell you everything on the way."

Now, I know the whole "don't go places with strangers" thing, but you have to realize that in the middle of all of this unreality, this guy made sense. I know it sounds bizarre, but he just felt right, and I knew I should trust him. Like I knew that he had been there waiting for me.

All right, yes. I can't say it didn't help that he was so darn sexy.

"Fine, I'll come with you, but only because I'm probably dreaming," I said.

He smiled, then motioned for me to follow him. I scurried to keep up with his long strides while I tried to untangle my hair and watch his cute butt at the same time. *You could bounce a quarter off of that thing! Oh my God. I sound like my mother. Talk about gross.* I almost ran into him when he came to an abrupt halt beside a florescent green car. "What is that?"

"A '76 Chevy Caprice," he said, opening the door for me.

"It looks like a giant green popsicle." I slid in onto the white leather seat, distracted by the vintage-ness of the old muscle car, while he went around and got in on the driver's side. I was just getting ready to open my mouth and tell him I had a thing for old cars too, when he leaned over and grabbed my arm.

Looking into my face, he said, "And you're not dreaming. You're dead."

෯෬

"Dead!" I tried to pull back from him. "What the hell?" My heart felt like it was going to pound out of my chest. Instead of letting me go, Alek pressed his body close to mine and wrapped me in his arms.

"Trust me. Let me show you," he said.

Like his voice was a drug, my body seemed to dissolve into him and I gasped as, still in his arms, I began to float above his Jell-O-colored car. White specks of light surrounded me. I looked up at Alek, who was drifting with me. His eyes glowed the red of a rising autumn moon.

Just like his eyes had been before . . . at the bus stop. Slowly, I began to remember as we floated through time back to the moment we'd first met.

He spoke, his voice whispering in my ear. "I was sent here to save you." His words were like mist. "Look down. Remember . . ."

I looked below us and saw everything. There I was, dressed in my LBD and my mom's hot but uncomfortable shoes, pouting and sullenly complaining to myself while I waited for the bus. There sat the three people crammed on the tiny bench, and then there was Alek, appearing from nowhere. I glanced questioningly at the Alek who floated with his arms around me. His eyes still burned hunter red, and they stilled the questions on my lips.

Watch . . . remember . . .

I looked down again and saw myself point Mr. Pepper at Alek's face. At those eyes that were just as red then as they were now. I could see myself yelling something, and at the same time I stepped back. It was then that mom's gorgeous stiletto heel missed the curb, and horrified, I saw my arms windmilling as I fell backward, hitting my head on the concrete with a sickening thud.

And that was it. I didn't move as the people at the bus stop surrounded me, obviously not knowing what to do. Through the middle of them walked Alek, but he was like a shadow in darkness. No one seemed to see him at all as he bent over my still body and whispered, "Your death was a gift, given by the ancients through me. You have been chosen. I am your teacher." Then he bent and covered my dead lips with his.

Okay, it was happening, but it wasn't. People were running around down there—literally walking *through* him while he kissed me. And even though they couldn't see him I could feel him. What he did to my dead body, I could now feel happening in my hovering soul as I drank in the exchange of death with life. I should have been terrified. I should have screamed or passed out or flailed against him. Instead I closed my eyes and let my soul absorb what I had seen. I accepted his gift and knew my world would never be the same.

❧❧❧

When I opened my eyes, I was back in the car pressed against Alek's chest. There were no sounds coming from inside of his muscular body, no breath, no heart thumping. I pulled back and stared at him.

"Are you even alive?"

My head felt funny, all kinda hummy and strange.

"I'm as alive as are you," he said. "You've just been changed. We're different. They used to call us vampires."

"Vampires?" I squeaked. "I have to drink blood?" I almost gagged just thinking about it.

He laughed softly. "It's not blood we drink—it's energy."

"Oh, God! We suck down electricity?" I frantically tried to remember who that chick was on old *Angel* reruns who zapped things with her electrically charged hands.

His strong arms were still around my waist and I wondered how they stayed so warm if he was dead. If *we* were dead. His smile was still in his eyes when he said, "No, it's not like that, either. You'll see."

His mouth was close to my ear. *Kiss me . . . kiss me again. . . .* His smiled widened and I felt my face burn with a blush. Could he read my mind?

"So we kinda match!" I blurted. *What?* As he chuckled at my dorkiness I pulled away and positioned myself back on my side of the car. This was depressing. With all this new power I could feel inside of me, I was still the same lame eighteen-year-old with no game.

"What was that?" Still smiling, Alek pulled his keys from his pocket and turned on the car, but for a moment I could swear disappointment flashed across his face. *Would he really have kissed me again if I hadn't gone all superdork on him and then vaulted to the other side of the car?*

"Yeah, umm, we match." I tried to stay as perky as I had been when I ruined the moment. "We're both strong, fearless creatures of night sent here to . . . do . . . stuff. What exactly do we do?"

"We all have different abilities." He cleared his throat in preparation, and I wondered how many times he had had this conversation. "I can affect time. That's how I got you to the bus stop, since you were taking too long getting there on your own, and that's also why you woke up today . . . again. Guess you could call that part a side effect. But, I'm not too sure what your ability is, but you'll figure it out pretty soon. It's the same for each of us, but different. You have to discover your own way. I was sent from below—"

"Hell?" I interrupted. "You came from Hell?"

"No. Or at least not your idea of Hell. Look, I was sent here to help you serve up vengeance on some and to save others."

"Like you saved me?"

"Well, kind of." He sighed and cleared his throat. "There are these ancient monsters whose spirits have been locked in the Underworld, and occasionally they find some way to escape. If they do, their only goals are to find a body and create the same chaos they did centuries ago. I'm the first of my kind, our kind, that were made to find these creatures and send them back. So, we're more like—"

"Monster-slaying superheroes?!" *Holy shit! What am I? A toddler?*

He laughed. "I guess you could call it that. I know where to take you, and we'll just wing it from there." He put the car in gear and started driving down the street.

Wing it? That didn't sound very reassuring.

I stared out the window, trying to make myself teleport or move things with my mind, when I noticed the reflection of my eyes. They were flashing from their normal plain brown to brilliant amber. That was good, right? I kept looking out the window and tried to concentrate. We passed a crowd of people leaving a late night movie when it happened again.

"Oh my God! That's it! I just thought it was part of me going crazy, but really it was my hidden superpower." I giddily turned to Alek, expecting him to know what I was talking about.

"What was your hidden power?"

"I can see stuff." It was just like with my mom, the weird vanilla smoke I'd seen around her. I leaned over Alek and pointed out the window to a cluster of people. "Like, I know that the girl in the pink cardigan and those really cute fuzzy boots is completely and totally in love, because I can see hot pink misty ribbons floating off of her. Oh, oh, and look at him." I pointed to a guy standing on the corner holding a WILL WORK FOR FOOD sign. "The smoke stuff around him is all brown and nasty. Hey! He has cancer." I paused, thinking hard, and suddenly *knew*. "He has lung cancer. He's gonna die. Soon." I shivered, not sure how I felt about my new superpower. Plopping myself back in my seat, I stared out the window and watched rainbows of smoke dance off people and twist through the autumn air, and *knew* things I simply shouldn't.

"That's good, you're learning already. There'll be more to come, though."

I closed my eyes and drew a long, shaky breath. *You're okay . . . you're okay. . . .*

"We're here." Alek turned off the car, and when I opened my eyes I half-expected to see creepy boat docks or a dark alley. Instead, we were in the middle of suburbia parked in front of a brick house identical to the ones on either side of it.

"You're kidding. This is the monster hideout where I'm supposed to fight crime?" Alek was already out of the car, and I hurried to catch up with him, following his longer legs up the driveway and past a very familiar SUV. "Hey!" He spun around and motioned for me to be quiet.

I lowered my voice, and spoke urgently. "But this is Paul's nerdy old Isuzu. He's dating my mom. Look, it has to be his SUV." I pointed at the window. "He has like fifty tacky evergreen air fresheners hanging from the rearview mirror because he smokes in his car and doesn't want my mom to notice." Obviously Alek didn't care, because he kept walking until he reached the side door and I had to scramble again to keep up.

"We're going in."

"What? Hell no! Didn't you just hear me? This is Paul's house and there's no way I'm going in there. Your monster radar is all wrong. Besides, he's on a date with my mom, and look, the lights aren't even on. They're probably not here, or worse. Ew. They might be—" Alek pressed one hand over my mouth and used the other to guide mine to the door.

"Can you feel that?" His hand lingered on mine and I wanted him to hold me like he had earlier.

Suddenly, the cold sluggishness of fear crept through the door and made ribbons up my arm. I tried to pull away, but Alek wouldn't let me. Rage and disgust followed. Their hot nails tore at my flesh, though the only marks they left were in my mind—on my soul. Alek let loose my hand and repeated, "We're going in there. Remember, trust me. I'm your protector."

As soon as he finished his sentence we were on the other side of the door. *I really wish he would warn me before he popped us places.* Alek nudged me toward the stairs and back into the reality I was trying unsuccessfully to escape. Like ghosts, we slid noiselessly up to the second floor. With each step the suffocating stench of smoky fear grew stronger. I wanted to vomit. At the top of the steps Alek took the lead. I let out a tiny sigh. Okay, right. He was my protector. Besides his superpower of zapping us places and kissing me into being a weird kind of vampire, he also must be super strong (as well as super hot). With him in front he could beat up any ancient boogey monster things lurking in the dark.

We walked into a room absent of all furniture except a metal table, the kind that morticians put dead bodies on. The cold room stank of bleach and blood, and the mixture became red and white ribbons of smoke that bit at my eyes. I scanned the room, amazed at how easily I could see through the smoke and shadows.

It was in one of those shadows that I saw her curly brown hair. I tore out from behind my protector and flew to her side. "Mom?!" The silence burned my ears. "Mom! Mom!" The soft vanilla I'd seen surrounding her earlier barely lingered within the rust-colored tendrils of hopelessness and panic, blinding me with fear. Tears washed my face, and my throat was hard and dry. "Alek, she's not moving. And I don't know what's wrong!" He was immediately at my side. I scrubbed at my eyes, wiping away tears and blinking through the otherworldly mists. He picked up my mother's limp body. She looked so unnaturally still and helpless it made my stomach roll. Mom was never helpless! She couldn't be!

"She's breathing. I'm sure she'll be fine." Alek began to reassure me, but like a bad horror movie, that was exactly when the predator entered.

"Oh, look. It's a party. Jenna, you didn't tell me you wanted to watch. That could have been arranged. I like an audience."

The man approaching me looked like the Paul I knew only briefly. Then my eyes grew hot and his body wavered, like heat rising from a hot summer road, and his true form was revealed to me. The smoke that swirled in and out of his body was terrible. It made his evil naked, and bared, he was fully exposed to me. I saw the sick creature he truly was. The souls of the people he had murdered shrieked purple ribbons of smoky agony from within him and tried to claw their way out from beneath his gray flesh. His eyes were fixed on me, but they wriggled in sockets swimming with parasites. Putrid lie-filled glop fell from his scorched lips and ate the ground where it landed.

Thanks to my new superpowers, I knew him for who he was—Alastor. A Greek demon who led others to sin and murder. *He's the serial killer, and he was hunting my mom.*

He had stopped moving toward us, and his body shimmered again, changing back into the Paul my mom had been tricked into caring about. "So, Mommy first, or you and your boyfriend?"

And it hit me. The rest of my new gift became clear. I turned to Alek, and in a commanding voice I barely recognized as my own I ordered, "Alek! Get her out of here! Call 911!"

Then I turned and faced the demon. "How about you start with me, asshole?" As I spoke I threw my arms wide and all of the tendrils of emotion swirling in the room rushed to me, wrapping around me, filling me with an incredible surge of power. I felt the dark emotions that had shimmered around Alastor enter my body and I knew the anger and hatred and awful strength of pure evil.

My mouth grew teeth I didn't know I had and my body began to vibrate with the power of the emotions I'd absorbed. I didn't think. I just felt and acted. I launched myself at the man my mother had trusted, wrapped my hands around his throat, and tried to tear off his suit of flesh. I had never felt so wild and so free. It was good to feel his flesh tear, to see his eyes bug out, to hear his whimper of terror. I was bloated with it, filled with darkness, and I wanted to rip him to pieces.

But before I could, Alek was pulling me from my opponent. He threw me against the wall so hard that, had I been alive, I would have surely died. By the time I shook off the shock and got to my feet, Alek had already finished him. He'd snapped his neck.

Let him off easy. I threw myself at Alek, knocking him back. My fangs cut into my bottom lip and the amber blood that trickled onto my tongue only made my rage grow as Alek regained his balance. But instead of hitting me back, he calmly wrapped his arms around my anger-bloated body, and held me tightly. The hollow sound of his chest and the autumn air that was his scent surrounded us, and like a cool fall rain following a baking hot summer, his presence washed the anger from me, leaving me so weak that I began to cry.

"You can't let it control you. That's where the horror stories of vampires came from—that's why so many of us have inspired bad B movies and the nightmares of humans. It's what happens to us when we lose control. If we let our powers overwhelm us, then we become the monsters we've been created to hunt." He set his chin on my head and I could feel him inhale the dried amber blood in my hair. "Feeding off him was enough. Don't let him taint you. You have to learn to keep the energy and let the evil go. His soul is back below in a far worse place than you could ever imagine, let that be punishment enough."

I looked up at him and suddenly understood. "You called yourself my protector, but you're not here to protect me from them. You're here to protect me from me."

"Yeah, that's right. Are you better now? Feel more like yourself?"

His voice was so deep, so incredibly gentle, and his eyes so warm that I lost myself in them. And then I saw the mist that surrounded him. It was a bright, brilliant amber—the same color as my blood. It reminded me of a clear and early dawn and new beginnings. The tendrils of gold wrapped around me, around us, and I couldn't help myself. I tiptoed and kissed him gently on the lips.

His blue eyes opened wide in surprise. Then he bent and kissed me back and I sank into him, finding my anchor, my center, my protector.

"Jenna, what's happening?"

At the sound of my mom's weak voice Alek and I sprang apart and I ran to where she lay just outside the room of death. I felt Alek move behind me, shielding her view of what used to be Paul.

"It's okay, Mom. It's gonna be fine," I said, reaching out to hold her and breathing a sigh of relief as I saw the vanilla mist that surrounded her, once more cream-colored and healthy, completely free of the taint of death.

ℬℭℜ

Alek stayed by my side, holding my hand and helping to strengthen me, keeping me from becoming overwhelmed by all of the tendrils of urgency, pain, and fear that surged with the presence of the police and EMTs and the neighbors who had started to mill around the front yard like worried sheep. He guided me to my mom, through the chaos that was invisible to everyone else but that I saw as mist within fog, so thick and swirling it was overwhelming. Mom was completely conscious, though she had a nasty bump on her head. I was still feeling a little sick with worry until I heard her tell an EMT that if she could just have a few Xanax and a glass of wine she'd be fixed right up and could go on home.

"Miss, you can ride with your mother if you'd like," the EMT called to me, still smiling at my mom's request for drugs and alcohol.

"Yeah, I'm coming," I said, then I turned to Alek. I looked into his blue eyes and saw a future so different than anything I could have dreamed that I suddenly felt shy. "Uh, I'm going to ride with her since, ya know, she's hurt." I giggled nervously. "Well, of course you do, you were—" He pulled me close and kissed my babbling lips. Leaves swept around my feet and wind rushed through my matted hair.

"I know." His breath tickled my nose. "I'll follow. You still have a lot to learn."

I jumped into the back of the ambulance and watched his cute butt as I walked all the way to his car. When he got to the bright green thing he looked back at me and his eyes glowed softly. "Hey," he called. "I think you were right before. I think we do match."

I grinned like a fool as the doors to the ambulance closed and my mom started pestering me with *who is that tall boy?* questions. As I tried to make up believable and not-get-me-in-trouble answers, I watched through the little glass windows while tendrils of caressing amber clung to the ambulance, guiding . . . protecting . . . ushering me into a whole new life.

Dead Man Stalking

A Morganville Vampires Story

RACHEL CAINE

iving in West Texas is sort of like living in Hell, but without the favorable climate and charming people. Living in Morganville, Texas, is all that and a takeout bag of worse. I should know. My name is Shane Collins, and I was born here, left here, came back here—none of which I had much choice about.

So, for you fortunate ones who've never set foot in this place, here's the walking tour of Morganville: It's home to a couple of thousand folks who breathe, and some crazy-ass number of people who don't. Vampires. Can't live with 'em, and in Morganville, you definitely can't live without 'em, because they run the town. Other than that, Morganville's a normal, dusty collection of buildings—the kind the oil boom of the '60s and '70s rolled by without dropping a dime in the banks. The university in the center of town acts like its own little city, complete with walls and gates.

Oh, and there's a secluded, tightly guarded vampire section of town too. I've been there, in chains. It's nice, if you're not looking forward to a horrible public execution.

I used to want to see this town burned to the ground, and then I had one of those things, what are they called, epiphanies? My epiphany was that one day I woke up and realized that if I lost Morganville and everybody in it . . . I'd have nothing at all. Everything I still cared about was here. Love it or hate it.

Epiphanies suck.

I was having another one of them on this particular day. I was sitting at a table inside Marjo's Diner, watching a dead man walk by the windows outside. Seeing dead men wasn't exactly unusual in Morganville; hell, one of my best friends is dead now, and he still gripes at me about doing the dishes. But there's vampire-dead, which Michael is, and then there's *dead*-dead, which was Jerome Fielder.

Except Jerome, dead or not, was walking by the window outside Marjo's.

"Order up," Marjo snapped, and slung my plate at me like a ground ball to third base; I stopped it from slamming into the wall by putting up my hand as a backstop. The bun of my hamburger slid over and onto the table—mustard side up, for a change.

"There goes your tip," I said. Marjo, already heading off to the next victim, flipped me off.

"Like you'd ever leave one, you cheap-ass punk."

I returned the gesture. "Don't you need to get to your second job?"

That made her pause, just for a second. "What second job?"

"I don't know, grief counselor? You being so sensitive and all."

That earned me another bird, ruder than the first one. Marjo had known me since I was a baby puking up formula. She didn't like me any better now than she had then, but that wasn't personal. Marjo didn't like anybody. Yeah, go figure on her entering the service industry.

"Hey," I said, and leaned over to look at her retreating bubble butt. "Did you just see who walked by outside?"

She turned to glare at me, round tray clutched in sharp red talons. "Screw you, Collins, I'm running a business here, I don't have time to stare out windows. You want something else or not?"

"Yeah. Ketchup."

"Go squeeze a tomato." She hustled off to wait another table—or not, as the mood took her.

I put veggies on my burger, still watching the parking lot outside the window. There were exactly six cars out there; one of them was my housemate Eve's, which I'd borrowed. The gigantic thing was really less a car than an ocean liner, and some days I called it the Queen Mary, and some days I called it Titanic, depending on how it was running. It stood out. Most of the other vehicles in the lot were crappy, sun-faded pickups and decrepit, half-wrecked sedans.

There was no sign of Jerome, or any other definitely dead guy, walking around out there now. I had one of those moments, those *did I really see that?* moments, but I'm not the delusional type. I had zero reason to imagine the guy. I didn't even *like* him, and he'd been dead for at least a year, maybe longer. Killed in a car wreck at the edge of town, which was code for *shot while trying to escape*, or the nearest Morganville equivalent. Maybe he'd pissed off his vampire Protector. Who knew?

Also, who cared? Zombies, vampires, whatever. When you live in Morganville, you learn to roll with the supernatural punches.

I bit into the burger and chewed. This was why I came to Marjo's . . . not the spectacular service, but the best hamburgers I'd ever eaten. Tender, juicy, spicy. Fresh, crisp lettuce and tomato, a little red onion. The only thing missing was . . .

"Here's your damn ketchup," Marjo said, and slid the bottle at me like a bartender in an old western saloon. I fielded it and saluted with it, but she was already moving on.

As I drizzled red on my burger, I continued to stare out the window. Jerome. That was a puzzle. Not enough to make me stop eating lunch, though.

Which shows you just how weird life in Morganville is, generally.

ℝℂℕ

I was prepared to forget all about Jerome, post-lunch, because not even Marjo's sour attitude could undo the endorphin high of her burger and besides, I had to get home. It was five o'clock. The bottling plant was letting out, and pretty soon the diner would be crowded with adults tired from a hard day's labor, and not many of them liked me any better than Marjo did. Most of them were older than me; at eighteen, I was starting to get the get-a-job-you-punk stares.

I like a good ass-kicking, but the Good Book is right: It's better to give than to receive.

I was unlocking the door to Eve's car when I saw somebody behind me on the window glass, blocking the blazing westerly sun. The reflection was smeared and indistinct, but in the ripples I made out some of the features.

Jerome Fielder. What do you know, I really *had* seen him.

I had exactly enough time to think, *Dude, say something witty*, before Jerome grabbed a handful of my hair and rammed me forehead-first into hot metal and glass. My knees went rubbery, and there was a weird high-pitched whine in my ears. The world went white, then pulsed red, then faded into darkness when he slammed me down again.

Why me? I had time to wonder, as it all went away.

❧❧❧

I woke up some time later, riding in the backseat of Eve's car and dripping blood all over the upholstery. *Oh, crap, she's gonna kill me for that*, I thought, which was maybe not the biggest problem I had. My wrists were tied behind my back, and Jerome had done some work on my ankles too. The bonds were so tight I'd lost feeling in both hands and feet, except for a slow, cold throb. I had a gash in my forehead, somewhere near the hairline I thought, and probably some kind of concussion thing, because I felt sick and dizzy.

Jerome was driving Eve's car, and I saw him watching me in the rearview mirror as we rattled along. Wherever we were, it was a rough road, and I bounced like a rag doll as the big tank of a car charged over bumps.

"Hey," I said. "So. Dead much, Jerome?"

He didn't say anything. That might have been because he liked me about as much as Marjo, but I didn't think so; he didn't look exactly *right*. Jerome had been a big guy, back in high school—big in the broad-shouldered sense. He'd been a gym worshipper, a football player, and winner of the biggest neck contest hands down.

Even though he still had all the muscles, it was like the air had been let out of them and now they were ropy and strangely stringy. His face had hollows, and his skin looked old and grainy.

Yep: dead guy. Zombified, which would have been a real mind-freak anywhere but Morganville; even in Morganville, though, it was weird. Vampires? Sure. Zombies? Not so you'd notice.

Jerome decided it was time to prove he still had a working voice box. "Not dead," he said. Just two words, and it didn't exactly prove his case because it sounded hollow and rusty. If I'd had to imagine a dead guy's voice, that would have been it.

"Great," I said. "Good for you. So, this car theft thing is new as a career move, right? And the kidnapping? How's that going for you?"

"Shut up."

He was absolutely right, I needed to do that. I was talking because hey, dead guy driving. It made me just a bit uncomfortable. "Eve's going to hunt you down and dismember you if you ding the car. Remember Eve?"

"Bitch," Jerome said, which meant he did remember. Of course he did. Jerome had been the president of the Jock Club and Eve had been the founder and nearly the only member of the Order of the Goth, Morganville Edition. Those two groups never got along, especially in the hothouse world of high school.

"Remind me to wash your mouth with soap later," I said, and shut my eyes as a particularly brutal bump bounced my head around. Red flashed through my brain, and I thought about things like aneurysms, and death. "Not nice to talk about people behind their backs."

"Go screw yourself."

"Hey, *three* words! You go, boy. Next thing you know, you'll be up to real sentences. . . . Where are we going?"

Jerome's eyes glared at me in the mirror some more. The car smelled like dirt, and something else. Something rotten. Skanky homeless unwashed clothes brewed in a vat of old meat.

I tried not to think about it, because between the smell and the lurching of the car and my aching head, well, you know. Luckily, I didn't have to not-think-about-it for long, because Jerome made a few turns and then hit the brakes with a little too much force.

I rolled off the bench seat and into the spacious legroom, and *ow*. "Ow," I made it official. "You learn that in Dead Guy Driver's Ed?"

"Shut up."

"You know, I think being dead might have actually given you a bigger vocabulary. You ought to think of suggesting that to the U. Put in an extension course or something."

The car shifted as Jerome got out of the front seat, and then the back door opened as he reached in to grab me under the arms and haul. Dead he might be; skanky, definitely. But still: strong.

Jerome dumped me on the caliche-white road, which was graded and graveled, but not recently, and walked off around the hood of the car. I squirmed and looked around. There was an old house about twenty feet away—the end of the pale road—and it looked weathered and defeated and sagging. Could have been a hundred years old, or five without maintenance. Hard to tell. Two stories, old-fashioned and square. Had one of those runaround porches people used to build to catch the cool breezes, although *cool* out here was relative.

I didn't recognize the place, which was a weird feeling. I'd grown up in Morganville, and I knew every nook and hiding place—survival skills necessary to making it to adulthood. That meant I wasn't *in* Morganville proper anymore. I knew there were some farmhouses outside of the town limits, but those who lived in them didn't come to town much, and nobody left the city without express vampire permission, unless they were desperate or looking for an easy suicide. So I had no idea who lived here. If anyone but Jerome did, these days.

Maybe he'd eaten all the former residents' brains, and I was his version of takeout. Yeah, that was comforting.

I worked on the ropes, but Jerome tied a damn good knot and my numbed fingers weren't exactly up to the task.

It had been quitting time at the plants when I'd gone out to the parking lot and ended up road kill, but now the big western sun was brushing the edge of the dusty horizon. Sunset was coming, in bands of color layered on top of each other, from red straight up to indigo.

I squirmed and tried to dislocate an elbow in order to get to my front pocket, where my cell phone waited patiently for me to text 911. No luck, and I ran out of time anyway.

Jerome came back around the car, grabbed me by the collar of my T-shirt, and pulled. I grunted and kicked and struggled like a fish on the line, but all that accomplished was to leave a wider drag-path in the dirt. I couldn't see where we were going. The backs of Jerome's fingers felt chilly and dry against my sweaty neck.

Bumpity-bump-bump up a set of steps that felt splinter-sharp even through my clothes, and the sunset got sliced off by a slanting dark roof. The porch was flatter, but no less uncomfortably splintered. I tried struggling again, this time really putting everything into it, but Jerome dropped me and smacked the back of my head into the wood floor. More red and white flashes, like my own personal emergency signal. When I blinked them away, I was being dragged across a threshold, into the dark.

Shit.

I wasn't up for bravado anymore. I was seriously scared, and I wanted out. My heart was pounding, and I was thinking of a thousand horrible ways I could die here in this stinking, hot, closed-up room. The carpet underneath my back felt stiff and moldy. What furniture there was looked abandoned and dusty, at least the stuff that wasn't in pieces.

Weirdly, there was the sound of a television coming from upstairs. Local news. The vampires' official mouthpieces were reporting safe little stories, world events, nothing too controversial. Talk about morphine for the masses.

The sound clicked off, and Jerome let go of me. I flopped over onto my side, then my face, and inchwormed my way up to my knees while trying not to get a mouthful of dusty carpet. I heard a dry rattle from behind me.

Jerome was laughing.

"Laugh while you can, monkey boy," I muttered, and spat dust. Not likely he'd ever seen *Buckaroo Banzai*, but it was worth a shot.

Footsteps creaked on the stairs from the second floor. I reoriented myself, because I wanted to be looking at whatever evil bastard was coming to the afternoon matinee of my probably gruesome death. . . .

Oh. Oh, *dammit.*

"Hello, son," my dad Frank Collins said. "Sorry about this, but I knew you wouldn't just come on your own."

ஸ்)Cℜ

The ropes came off, once I promised to be a good boy and not rabbit for the car the second I had the chance. My father looked about the same as I'd expected, which meant not good but strong. He'd started out a random pathetic alcoholic; after my sister had died—accident or murder, you take your pick—he'd gone off the deep end. So had my mom. So had I, for that matter.

Sometime in there, my dad had changed from random pathetic drunk to mean, badass vampire-hunting drunk. The vampire-hating component of that had been building up for years, and it had exploded like an ancient batch of TNT when my mother died—by suicide, maybe. I didn't believe it, and neither did my dad. The vampires had been behind it, like they were behind every terrible thing that had ever happened in our lives.

That's what I used to believe, anyway. And what Dad still did.

I could smell the whiskey rising up off of him like the bad-meat smell off of Jerome, who was kicked back in a chair in the corner, reading a book. Funny. Jerome hadn't been much of a reader when he'd been alive.

I sat obligingly on the ancient, dusty couch, mainly because my feet were too numb to stand, and I was trying to work circulation back into my fingers. Dad and I didn't hug. Instead, he paced, raising dust motes that glimmered in the few shafts of light that fought their way through smudged windows.

"You look like crap," Dad said, pausing to stare at me. I resisted the urge, like Marjo, to give him a one-fingered salute, because he'd only beat the crap out of me for it. Seeing him gave me a black, sick feeling in the pit of my stomach. I wanted to love him. I wanted to hit him. I didn't know what I wanted, except that I wanted this whole thing to just go away.

"Gee, thanks, Dad," I said, and deliberately slumped back on the couch, giving him all the teen attitude I could. "I missed you too. I see you brought all your friends with you. Oh, wait."

The last time my dad had rolled into Morganville, he'd done it in a literal kind of way—on a motorcycle, with a bunch of badass motorcycle biker buddies. No sign of them this time. I wondered when they'd finally told him to shove it, and how hard.

Dad didn't answer. He kept staring at me. He was wearing a leather jacket with lots of zippers, faded blue jeans, sturdy boots. Not too different from what I was wearing, minus the jacket, because only a stupid jerk would be in leather in this heat. Looking at *you*, Dad.

"Shane," he said. "You knew I'd come back for you."

"Yeah, that's really sweet. The last time I saw you, you were trying to blow my ass up along with a whole building full of vampires, remember? What's my middle name, Collateral Damage?" He'd have done it too. I knew my dad too well to think anything else. "You also left me to burn alive in a cage, *Dad*. So excuse me if I'm not getting all misty-eyed while the music swells."

His expression—worn into a hard leather mask by wind and sun—didn't change. "It's a war, Shane. We talked about this."

"Funny thing, I don't remember you saying, *If you get caught by the vampires, I'll leave you to burn, dumbass*. But maybe I'm just not remembering all the details of your clever plan." Feeling was coming back into my fingers and toes. Not fun. It felt like I'd dipped them in battery acid and then rolled them in lye. "I can get over that. But you had to go and drag my friends into it."

That was what I hated the most. Sure, he'd screwed me over—more than once, actually. But he was right, we'd kind of agreed that one or the other of us might have to bite it for the cause, back when I believed in his cause.

We hadn't agreed about innocent people, especially my friends, getting thrown on the pile of bodies.

"Your *friends*, right," Dad said, with about a bottle's worth of cheap whiskey emphasis. "A half-vampire, a wannabe morbid freak, and—oh, you mean that girl, don't you? The little skinny one. She melted the brains right out of your head, didn't she? I warned you about that."

Claire. He didn't even remember her name. I closed my eyes for a second, and there she was, smiling up at me with those clear, trusting eyes. She might be small, but she had a kind of strength my dad wouldn't ever understand. She was the first really pure thing that I'd ever known, and I wasn't about to let him take her away. She was waiting for me right now, back at the Glass House, probably studying and chewing a pencil. Or arguing with Eve. Or . . . wondering where the hell I was.

I had to get out of this. I had to get back to Claire.

Painful or not, my feet were functional again. I tested them by standing up. In the corner, Dead Jerome put aside his book. It was a battered, water-stained copy of *The Wizard of Oz*. Who did he think he was? The Cowardly Lion? The Scarecrow? Hell, maybe he thought he was Dorothy.

"Just like I thought, this is all about the girl. You probably think you're some knight in shining armor come to save her." Dad's smile was sharp enough to cut diamonds. "You know how she sees you? A big, dumb idiot she can put on a leash. Her own pet pit bull. Your innocent little schoolgirl, she's wearing the Founder's symbol now. She's working for the vampires. I sure as hell hope she's like a porn star in the sack for you to be betraying your own like this."

This time, I didn't need a knock on the head to see red. I felt my chin going down, my lungs filling, but I held on to my temper. Somehow.

He was trying to make me charge him.

"I love her, Dad," I said. "Don't."

"Love, yeah, right. You don't know the meaning of the word, Shane. She's working for the leeches. She's helping them regain control of Morganville. She has to go, and you know it."

"Over my dead body."

In the corner, Jerome laughed that scratchy, raspy laugh that made me want to tear out his voice box once and for all. "Could be arranged," he croaked.

"Shut up," my dad snapped without taking his eyes off of me. "Shane, listen to me. I've found the answer."

"Wait—let me guess—forty-two?" No use. Dad wasn't anywhere near cool enough to be a Douglas Adams fan. "I don't care what you've found, Dad, and I'm not listening to you anymore. I'm going home. You want to have your pet dead guy stop me?"

His eyes fixed on my wrist, where I was wearing a bracelet. Not one of those things that would have identified me as vamp property—a hospital bracelet, white plastic with a big red cross on it.

"You wounded?" Not, of course, was I sick. I was just another foot soldier, to Dad. You were either wounded, or malingering.

"Whatever. I'm better," I said.

It seemed, for just a second, that he softened. Maybe nobody but me would have noticed. Maybe I imagined it too. "Where were you hurt, boy?"

I shrugged and pointed to my abs, slightly off to one side. The scar still ached and felt hot. "Knife."

He frowned. "How long ago?"

"Long enough." The bracelet would be coming off in the next week. My grace period was nearly over.

He looked into my eyes, and for a second, just a second, I let myself believe he was genuinely concerned.

Sucker.

He always had been able to catch me off guard, no matter how carefully I watched him, and I didn't even see the punch coming until it was too late. It was hard, delivered with surgical precision, and it doubled me over and sent me stumbling back to flop onto the couch again. *Breathe*, I told my muscles. My solar plexus told me to stuff it, and my insides throbbed, screaming in pain and terror. I heard myself making hard, gasping noises, and hated myself for it. *Next time. Next time I hit the bastard first.*

I knew better, though.

Dad grabbed me by the hair and yanked my head back. He pointed my face in Jerome's direction. "I'm sorry, boy, but I need you to *listen* right now. You see him? *I brought him back, right out of the grave.* I can bring them all back, as many as I need. They'll fight for me, Shane, and they won't quit. It's time. We can take this town back, and we can finally end this nightmare."

My frozen muscles finally unclenched, and I pulled in a whooping, hoarse gasp of air. Dad let go of my hair and stepped away.

He'd always known when to back off too.

"Your definition of—the end of the nightmare—is a little different—from mine," I wheezed. "Mine doesn't include zombies." I swallowed and tried to slow my heart rate. "How'd you do it, Dad? How the hell is he standing here?"

He brushed that aside. Of course. "I'm trying to explain to you that it's time to quit talking about the war, and time to start fighting it. We can win. We can destroy all of them." He paused, and the glow in his eyes was the next best thing to a fanatic with a bomb strapped to his chest. "I need you, son. We can do it together."

That part, he really meant. It was sick and twisted, but he did need me.

And I needed to use that. "First, tell me how you do it," I said. "I need to know what I'm signing up for."

"Later." Dad clapped me on the shoulder. "When you're convinced this is necessary, maybe. For now, all you need to know is that it's possible, I've done it. Jerome's proof."

"No, Dad. Tell me how. Either I'm in it or I'm not. No more secrets."

Nothing I was saying was going to register with him as a lie, because they weren't lies. I was saying what he wanted to hear. First rule of growing up with an abusive father: you cope, you bargain, you learn how to avoid getting hit.

And my father wasn't bright enough to know I'd figured it out.

Still, some instinct warned him; he looked at me with narrowed eyes, a frown wrinkling his forehead. "I'll tell you," he said. "But you need to show me you can be trusted first."

"Fine. Tell me what you need." That translated into, *Tell me who you need me to beat up.* As long as I was willing to do that, he'd believe me.

I was hoping it would be Jerome.

"Of everybody who died in the last couple of years, who was the strongest?"

I blinked, not sure it was a trick question. "Jerome?"

"Besides Jerome."

"I guess—probably Tommy Barnes." Tommy was no teenager; he'd been in his thirties when he'd kicked it, and he'd been a big, mean, tough dude even the other big, mean, tough dudes had given a wide berth. He'd died in a bar fight, I'd heard. Knifed from behind. He'd have snapped the neck off of anybody who'd tried it to his face.

"Big Tom? Yeah, he'd do." Dad nodded thoughtfully. "All right, then. We're bringing him back."

The last person on Earth I'd want to bring back from the grave would be Big Tommy Barnes. He'd been crazy-badass alive. I could only imagine death wouldn't have improved his temper.

But I nodded. "Show me."

Dad took off his leather jacket, and then stripped off his shirt. In contrast to the sun-weathered skin of his arms, face, and neck, his chest was fish-belly white, and it was covered with tattoos. I remembered some of them, but not all the ink was old.

He'd recently had our family portrait tattooed over his heart.

I forgot to breathe for a second, staring at it. Yeah, it was crude, but those were the lines of Mom's face, and Alyssa's. I didn't realize, until I saw them, that I'd nearly forgotten how they looked.

Dad looked down at the tat. "I needed to remind myself," he said.

My throat was so dry that it clicked when I swallowed. "Yeah." My own face was there, frozen in indigo blue at the age of maybe sixteen. I looked thinner, and even in tattoo form I looked more hopeful. More sure.

Dad held out his right arm, and I realized that there was more new ink.

And this stuff was *moving*.

I took a step back. There were dense, strange symbols on his arm, all in standard tattoo ink, but there was nothing standard about what the tats were doing—namely, they were revolving slowly like a DNA helix up and down the axis of his arm, under the skin. "*Christ, Dad*—"

"Had it done in Mexico," he said. "There was an old priest there, he knew things from the Aztecs. They had a way to bring back the dead, so long as they hadn't been gone for more than two years, and were in decent condition otherwise. They used them as ceremonial warriors." Dad flexed his arm, and the tattoos flexed with him. "This is part of what does it."

I felt sick and cold now. This had moved way past what I knew. I wished wildly that I could show this to Claire; she'd probably be fascinated, full of theories and research.

She'd know what to do about it.

I swallowed hard and said, "And the other part?"

"That's where you come in," Dad said. He pulled his T-shirt on again, hiding the portrait of our family, "I need you to prove you're up for this, Shane. Can you do that?"

I gulped air and finally, convulsively nodded. *Play for time,* I was telling myself. *Play for time, think of something you can do.* Short of chopping off my own father's arm, though. . . .

"This way," Dad said. He went to the back of the room. There was a door there, and he'd added a new, sturdy lock to it that he opened with a key from his jacket.

Jerome gave me that creepy laugh again, and I felt my skin shiver into gooseflesh.

"Right. This might be a shock," Dad said. "But trust me, it's for a good cause."

He swung open the door and flipped on a harsh overhead light.

It was a windowless cell, and inside, chained to the floor with thick silver-plated links, was a vampire.

Not just any vampire. Oh no, that would have been too easy for my father.

It was Michael Glass, my best friend.

Michael looked—white. Paler than pale. I'd never seen him look like that. There were burns on his arms, big raised welts where the silver was touching, and there were cuts. He was leaking slow trickles of blood on the floor.

His eyes were usually blue, but now they were red, bright red. Scary monster red, like nothing human.

But it was still my best friend's voice whispering, "Help."

I couldn't answer him. I backed up and slammed the door.

Jerome was laughing again, so I turned around, picked up a chair, and smashed him in the face with it. I could have hit him with a powder puff, for all the good it did. He grabbed the chair, broke the thick wood with a snap of his hands, and threw it back at me. I stumbled, and would have gone down except for the handy placement of a wall.

"Stop. Don't touch my son," my father said. Jerome froze like he'd run into a brick wall, hands working like he still wanted to rip out my throat.

I turned on my dad and snarled, "That's my friend!"

"No, that's a vampire," he said. "The youngest one. The weakest one. The one most of them won't come running to rescue."

I wanted to scream. I wanted to punch somebody. I felt pressure building up inside, and my hands were shaking. "What the hell are you doing to him?"

I didn't know who he was, this guy in the leather jacket looking at me. He looked like a tired, middle-aged biker, with his straggly graying hair, his sallow, seamed face, his scars and tats. Only his eyes seemed like they belonged to my dad, and even then, only for a second.

"It's a vampire," he said. "It's not your friend, Shane. You need to be real clear about that—your friend is dead, just like Jerome here, and you can't let that get in the way of what needs to be done. When we go to war, we get them all. *All.* No exceptions."

Michael had played at our house. My dad had tossed a ball around with him and pushed his swing and served him cake at birthday parties.

And my dad didn't care about any of that anymore.

"How?" My jaw felt tight. I was grinding my teeth, and my hands were shaking. "How did you do this? What are you doing to him?"

"I'm bleeding it and storing the blood, just like they do us humans," Dad said. "It's a two-part spell—the tattoo, and the blood of a vampire. It's just a creature, Shane. Remember that."

Michael wasn't a creature. Not *just* a creature, anyway; neither was what Dad had pulled out of Jerome's grave, for that matter. Jerome wasn't just a mindless killing machine. Mindless killing machines didn't fill their spare time with the adventures of Dorothy and Toto. They didn't even know they *had* spare time. I could see it in Jerome's wide, yellowed eyes now. The pain. The terror. The anger.

"Do you want to be here?" I asked him, straight out.

For just that second, Jerome looked like a boy. A scared, angry, hurt little boy. "No," he said. "Hurts."

I wasn't going to let this happen. Not to Michael, oh hell no. And not even to Jerome.

"Don't you go all soft on me, Shane. I've done what needed doing," Dad said. "Same as always. You used to be weak. I thought you'd manned up."

Once, that would have made me try to prove it by fighting something. Jerome, maybe. Or him.

I turned and looked at him and said, "I really would be weak, if I fell for that tired bullshit, Dad." I raised my hands, closed them into fists, and then opened them again and let them fall. "I don't need to prove anything to you. Not anymore."

I walked out the front door, out to the dust-filmed black car. I popped the trunk and took out a crowbar.

Dad watched me from the door, blocking my way back into the house. "What the hell are you doing?"

"Stopping you."

He threw a punch as I walked up the steps toward him. This time, I saw it coming, saw it telegraphed clearly in his face before the impulse ever reached his fist.

I stepped out of the way, grabbed his arm, and shoved him face-first into the wall. "Don't." I held him there, pinned like a bug on a board, until I felt his muscles stop fighting me. The rest of him never would. "We're done, Dad. Over. This is *over.* Don't make me hurt you, because God, I really want to."

I should have known he wouldn't just give up.

The second I let him go, he twisted, jammed an elbow into my abused stomach, and forced me backward. I knew his moves by now, and sidestepped an attempt to hook my feet out from under me.

"Jerome!" Dad yelled. "Stop my—"

The end of that sentence was going to be *son,* and I couldn't let him put Jerome back in the game or this was over before it started.

So I punched my father full in the face. Hard. With all the rage and resentment that I'd stored up over the years, and all the anguish, and all the fear. The shock rattled every bone in my body, and my whole hand sent up a red flare of distress. My knuckles split open.

Dad hit the floor, eyes rolling back in his head. I stood there for a second, feeling oddly cold and empty, and saw his eyelids flutter.

He wouldn't be out for long.

I moved quickly across the room, past Jerome, who was still frozen in place, and opened the door to the cell. "Michael?" I crouched down across from him, and my friend shook gold hair back from his white face and stared at me with eerie, hungry eyes.

I held up my wrist, showing him the bracelet. "Promise me, man. I get you out of here, no biting. I love you, but no."

Michael laughed hoarsely. "Love you too, bro. Get me the hell out of here."

I set to work with the crowbar, pulling up floorboards and gouging the eyebolts out for each set of chains. I'd been right; my dad was too smart to make chains out of solid silver. Too soft, too easy to break. These were silver-plated—good enough to do the job on Michael, if not one of the older vamps.

I only had to pull up the first two; Michael's vampire strength took care of yanking the others from the floor.

Michael's eyes flared red when I leaned closer, trying to help him up, and before I knew what was happening, he'd wrapped a hand around my throat and slammed me down, on my back, on the floor. I felt the sting of sharp nails in my skin, and saw his eyes fixed on the cut on my head.

"No biting," I said again, faintly. "Right?"

"Right," Michael said, from somewhere out beyond Mars. His eyes were glowing like storm lanterns, and I could feel every muscle in his body trembling. "Better get that cut looked at. Looks bad."

He let me up, and moved with about half his usual vampire speed to the door. Dad might not let Jerome have at me, but he wasn't going to hold back with Michael, and Michael was—at best—half his normal strength right now. Not exactly a fair fight.

"Michael," I said, and put my back against the wall next to him. "We go together, straight to the window. You get out, don't wait for me. The sun should be down far enough that you can make it to the car." I gathered up a handful of silver chain and wrapped it around my hand. "Don't even think about arguing right now."

He sent me an are-you-kidding look, and nodded.

We moved fast, and together. I got in Jerome's way and delivered a punch straight from the shoulder right between his teeth, reinforced with silver-plated metal.

I only intended to knock him back, but Jerome howled and stumbled, hands up to ward me off. It was like years fell away, and all of a sudden we were back in junior high again—him the most popular bully in school, me finally getting enough size and muscle to stand up to him. Jerome had made that same girly gesture the first time I'd hit back.

It threw me off.

A crossbow bolt fired from the far corner of the living room hissed right over my head and slammed to a vibrating stop in the wooden wall. "Stop!" Dad ordered hoarsely. He was on his knees, but he was up and very, very angry. He was also reloading, and the next shot wouldn't be a warning.

"Get out!" I screamed at Michael, and if he was thinking about staging a reenactment of the gunfight at the OK Corral, he finally saw sense. He jumped through the nearest window in a hail of glass and hit the ground running. I'd been right: The sun was down, or close enough that it wouldn't hurt him too badly.

He made it to the car, opened the driver's side door, and slid inside. I heard the roar as the engine started. "Shane!" he yelled. "Come on!"

"In a second," I yelled back. I stared at my father, and the moving tattoo. He had the crossbow aimed right at my chest. I twirled the crowbar in one hand, the silver chain in the other. "So," I said, watching my father. "Your move, Dad. What now? You want me to do a cage match with Dead Jerome? Would that make you happy?"

My dad was staring not at me, but at Dead Jerome, who was cowering in the corner. I'd hurt him, or the silver had; half his face was burned and rotting, and he was weeping in slow, retching sobs.

I knew the look Dad was giving him. I'd seen it on my father's face more times than I could count. Disappointment.

"My *son*," Dad said in disgust. "You ruin everything."

"I guess Jerome's more your son than I am," I said. I walked toward the front door. I wasn't going to give my father the satisfaction of making me run. I knew he had the crossbow in his hands, and I knew it was loaded.

I knew he was sighting on my back.

I heard the trigger release, and the ripped-silk hiss of wood traveling through air. I didn't have time to be afraid, only—like my dad—bitterly disappointed.

The crossbow bolt didn't hit me. Didn't even miss me.

When I turned, at the door, I saw that he'd put the crossbow bolt, tipped with silver, through Jerome's skull. Jerome slid silently down to the floor. Dead. Finally, mercifully dead.

The *Wizard of Oz* fell face down next to his hand.

"Son," my dad said, and put the crossbow aside. "Please, don't go. I need you. I really do."

I shook my head.

"This thing—it'll only last another few days," he said. "The tattoo. It's already fading. I don't have *time* for this, Shane. It has to be now."

"Then I guess you're out of luck."

He snapped the crossbow up again.

I ducked to the right, into the parlor, jumped the wreckage of a couch, and landed on the cracked, curling floor of the old kitchen. It smelled foul and chemical in here, and I spotted a fish tank on the counter, filled with cloudy liquid. Next to it was a car battery.

DIY silver plating equipment, for the chains.

There was also a 1950s-era round-shouldered fridge, rattling and humming.

I opened it.

Dad had stored Michael's blood in bottles, old dirty milk bottles likely scavenged from the trash heap in the corner. I grabbed all five bottles and threw them one at a time out the window, aiming for a big upthrusting rock next to a tree.

Smash. Smash. Smash. Smash . . .

"Stop," Dad spat. In my peripheral vision I saw him standing there, aiming his reloaded crossbow at me. "I'll kill you, Shane. I swear I will."

"Yeah? Lucky you've already got me tattooed on your chest, then, with the rest of the dead family." I pulled back for the throw.

"I could bring back your mother," Dad blurted. "Maybe even your sister. Don't."

Oh, *God*. Sick black swam across my vision for a second.

"You throw that bottle," he whispered, "and you're killing their last chance to live."

I remembered Jerome—his sagging muscles, his grainy skin, the panic and fear in his eyes.

Do you want to be here?

No. Hurts.

I threw the last bottle of Michael's blood and watched it sail straight and true, to shatter in a red spray against the rock.

I thought he'd kill me. Maybe *he* thought he'd kill me too. I waited, but he didn't pull the trigger.

"I'm fighting for humanity," he said. His last, best argument. It had always won me over before.

I turned and looked him full in the face. "I think you already lost yours."

I walked out past him, and he didn't stop me.

❧❧❧

Michael drove like a maniac, raising contrails of caliche dust about a mile high as we sped back to the main highway. He kept asking me how I was doing. I didn't answer him, just looked out at the gorgeous sunset, and the lonely, broken house fading in the distance.

We blasted past the Morganville city limits sign, and one of the ever-lurking police cars cut us off. Michael slowed, stopped, and turned off the engine. A rattle of desert wind shook the car.

"Shane."

"Yeah."

"He's dangerous."

"I know that."

"I can't just let this go. Did you see—"

"I saw," I said. "I know." *But he's still my father,* some small, frightened kid inside me wailed. *He's all I have.*

"Then what do you want me to say?" Michael's eyes had faded back to blue, now, but he was still white as a ghost, blue-white, scary-white. I'd spilled all his blood out there on the ground. The burns on his hands and wrists made my stomach clench.

"Tell them the truth," I said. If the Morganville vampires got to my dad before he could get the hell out, he'd die horribly, and God knew, he probably deserved it. "But give him five minutes, Michael. Just five."

Michael stared at me, and I couldn't tell what was in his mind at all. I'd known him most of my life, but in that long moment, he was just as much of a stranger as my father had been.

A uniformed Morganville cop tapped on the driver's side window. Michael rolled it down. The cop hadn't been prepared to find a vampire driving, and I could see him amending the harsh words he'd been about to deliver.

"Going a little fast, sir," he finally said. "Something wrong?"

Michael looked at the burns on his wrists, the bloodless slices on his arms. "Yeah," he said. "I need an ambulance."

And then he slumped forward, over the steering wheel. The cop let out a squawk of alarm and got on his radio. I reached out to ease Michael back. His eyes were shut, but as I stared at him, he murmured, "You wanted five minutes."

"I wasn't looking for a Best Supporting Actor award!" I muttered back.

Michael did his best impression of Vampire in a Coma for about five minutes, and then came to and assured the cop and arriving ambulance attendants he was okay.

Then he told them about my dad.

They found Jerome, still and evermore dead, with a silver-tipped arrow through his head. They found a copy of *The Wizard of Oz* next to him.

There was no sign of Frank Collins.

Later that night—around midnight—Michael and I sat outside on the steps of our house. I had a bottle of most illegal beer; he was guzzling his sixth bottle of blood, which I pretended not to notice. He had his arm around Eve, who had been pelting us both with questions all night in a nonstop machine gun patter; she'd finally run down, and leaned against Michael with sleepy contentment.

Well, she hadn't *quite* run down. "Hey," she said, and looked up at Michael with big, dark-rimmed eyes. "Seriously. You can bring back dead guys with *vampire juice*? That is so wrong."

Michael almost spit out the blood he was swallowing. "*Vampire juice*? Damn, Eve. Thanks for your concern."

She lost her smile. "If I didn't laugh, I'd scream."

He hugged her. "I know. But it's over."

Next to me, Claire had been quiet all night. She wasn't drinking—not that we'd have let her, at sixteen—and she wasn't saying much, either. She also wasn't looking at me. She was staring out at the Morganville night.

"He's coming back," she finally said. "Your dad's not going to give it up, is he?"

I exchanged a look with Michael. "No," I said. "Probably not. But it'll be a while before he gets his act together again. He expected to have me to help him kick off his war, and like he said, his time was running out. He'll need a brand-new plan."

Claire sighed and linked her arm through mine. "He'll find one."

"He'll have to do it without me." I kissed the soft, warm top of her hair.

"I'm glad," she said. "You deserve better."

"News flash," I said. "I've *got* better. Right here."

Michael and I clinked glasses, and toasted our survival.

However long it lasted.

Table Manners

TANITH LEE

*T*he moment I saw him I knew. I suppose any one of us would, by now. We're so used, via movie and novel, to the nature and ways of The Vampire (capital letters intended), we can—or ought to—spot one at two hundred paces. And go grab ourselves a sharpened stake—

Or, of course, not . . .

I had been sent, that is *persuaded*, to attend the October Ball at the Reconstruct Mansion, by my father, Anthony. He said, and here I quote: "You'll find it interesting, I think."

"Why?" I had demanded. For this wasn't how I wished to spend the first five days of the month.

"Because the world is full of people like the Kokersons. If you like, Lel, put this down as the final part of your education. You'll learn how such people tick."

"Tick in the sense," I said, "of clock or bomb?"

"Either," replied my elegant, lovely, and infuriating father.

October is fall. Time of flaming, *falling* leaves, of mists and dreams, before Halloween and winter close in. I'd had my own plans, but there you go. Dad knows it all. (The trouble is, as far as I can tell, he usually does.)

And so I accepted the Kokerson invite and packed my bags and caught the train to Chakhatti Halt, and then took a cab driven by a very sweet guy, who looked and spoke just like a really jolly Tyrannosaurus Rex (I do not lie) in (quasi-) human form.

I call the castle Reconstruct Mansion, did so from the very start, the moment I read in a newspaper that they had imported the edifice, once a huge old castle-type house from someplace in Eastern Europe, and were having it rebuilt stone by stone, in a vast parkland some other place, well outside the small town of Chakhatti. The Kokersons, obviously, are very rich. One of them won a lottery about twenty years back. I had seen photos of them. I really didn't want to go. But go there, Anthony thought I must.

In case this makes my dad sound like a manipulative monster I have to state right here and now that is the very opposite of what he is. As I said, it's just—he seems to know about . . . everything. But then, that's how he is.

My name is Lelystra. It's a family name, only usually I have myself called Lel by those who are my friends. Call me Lel, all right?

✺⟫⟨⟪

"Oh! You should have called—we would have sent a car! And you are Lelystra? What a delicious name! Oh, we wouldn't *dream* of mangling it down to *Lel*!!!"

So they greeted me, the Kokersons. A never-ending family, only lacking a father (had he run away? I might have). Toothy, bronzed sons and toothy, bleached daughters, and boisterous aunts, and an uncle like a dark satanic Bill (his name), and the mother, Mrs. Kokerson, or Ariadne, as I was told to call her. She was fifteen going on sixty. That is, she *was* sixty, but had somehow stayed fifteen in all the *wrong* ways. I felt an immediate requirement to look after her, steer her away from the cocktails—she was *much* too young to even taste one—and perhaps introduce her to some youthfully elderly male.

I flew upstairs with wings of worry on my feet and leapt into the cover of a bright white bedroom, with a bed the size of a softball field.

I tried to put through a call to Anthony. Cunningly he was in a meeting. I left a message. "Dad, I am going to kill you."

∽)Q∂

Let me describe the reconstruct castle.

An apparent ascending thousand feet of coal-blue stone, with towers, cupolas, balconies, verandas, staircases inside and out like static stepped waterfalls, and some of them just as slippery. The window glass is lightly polarized. From outside the windows look like smoky eyeglasses. Inside they color day sky green, and night sky purple, with pink stars. The landscape all around is private and full of trees, lake, and deer. October stags bellowed from the woods all night, waking me regular as a fire alarm roughly every thirty minutes.

It was all a gigantic theme park.

The *theme*, presumably, was the Kokersons, or their fantasy about themselves. The feel of fake antiquity and illusory age was so intense it was quite serious.

And we all had to dress in the clothes they provided, females in flowing gowns, males in gothic tailoring, nothing later than 1880, or earlier than 1694. We were like refugees from a muddled movie set. Even the house was like that.

Two days, two bellowing nights passed.

∽)Q∂

The day of the ball, everyone (or the Young People, at least) spent all morning and afternoon compulsorily in hot tubs, being massaged, creamed, pedicure-manicured, topped off by shampoo and styling (as if for a cat show). Then came the dressing up in the most extreme clothes yet.

I yawned and yawned, blaming it on the wake-up calls of the noisy stags.

My dress, which Ariadne had chosen me, was white. (Ariadne: "So perfect with your lovely pale hair.") My hair is natural, but somehow the hairdresser had gotten it to go even paler—scared it, maybe. My skin is white too. I like the sun but never take a tan. In the white dress I vanished without meaning to, became a sort of plaster statue figure lacking any features, apart from my eyes which, thank the Lord, are very dark gray.

I thought, *I shall attend, play their silly game, dance a few of the minuets and waltzes* (anything modern was absolutely out), *and retire graciously soon as I can, later saying I was still there all the while.* I'm good at that sort of thing.

Either that is selfishly self-protective, or my kinder side not wanting to offend or hurt. I have no idea which and I don't care. It works. I escape, others aren't upset.

So I descended the indoor glass-slippery, glass-slipper stair, and entered the ballroom (like the outside of a bridal cake, icing sugar and gilding, with grapevines of chandeliers). I glanced around.

And that was when I saw him. And knew him. Or rather, knew what he *was*.

And all along my spine, rising upward, ran the kind of prickly electricity that on a cat reveals itself as the fur standing on end.

Ariadne sailed by, right on cue.

Me, casually: "Who is that? I *do* like his costume."

"Yes, isn't it glorious? But I'm sure you notice that he's *very* handsome too," she enthused at me.

I answered calmly. "Yes. Quite a good face."

"And *perfect* masculine physique. Strong, like a dancer's. And his hair—"

"Is it really so long or is that a piece?"

"No. It's all his own. It's only that usually Anghel ties it back. How romantic he looks, doesn't he? I'm not surprised you'd pick him out. But I have to warn you, Lelystra, he's cold as snow. Cold as—" She fought for an even more cryogenic noun.

"As very *cold* snow?" I helpfully suggested.

"Well, er, yes. The *coldest* of cold snow. We're all quite crazy over him, and my two daughters are besotted, but he's only ever polite. But then, Anghel has escorted *movie stars*. Always in demand. He only arrived an hour ago."

"Really."

"He's been offered parts himself in so many movies—"

"But always coldly and politely refused," I supplied. I tried to keep all trace of irritation from my voice. *Obviously* he wouldn't take a part in any film. You only had to look at him to see it—this one would never be up at the crack of dawn and out on location in the blazing sun.

He was A Vampire.

Someone called Ariadne then, and she floated off on a sea of people dancing polkas.

Anghel (a name to conjure with) might be any age from twenty to six hundred. Or more. He looked about twenty-two. His hair was black as if he had washed it in the night outside. His eyes were blacker. He was pale, paler no doubt than I was. It wasn't any kind of make-up. He had a handsome—no, a beautiful—and cruel face. It was his mask, evidently, to keep all of us just far enough away—or if near then suitably nervous and/or impressed—while he chose his victim for that night, maybe for the weekend. It wouldn't be more, because also evidently he hadn't *killed* anyone by drinking their blood. His dates might keep quiet, or be made to "forget" what had gone on, but surely word would have gotten around if none of them ever went home. His quaint costume was that of some European nobleman of the eighteenth century. All black, need I add, and embroidered, the tall black boots flittering with quills of steel and his coat with wild lace cuffs of sheerest snow white (to match his manner, perhaps).

He was unmistakable!

I felt I should have known he'd be here, been *warned*. Maybe I took my ignorance too much to heart.

Yet my—almost *outrage*—made me linger after all. None of the rest of them, it seemed, could figure him out, and put their fascination down only to his looks. I had to assume too that now and then, if only after dark, he had been spotted in everyday garb where, frankly, even if his hair *was* tied back, and he wore jeans and a baseball cap to advertize the Chakhatti Arrows, he would stick out like an eagle in an aviary of pigeons.

I am not ashamed of what I next did. I felt it was my right and duty. If everyone else was blind, I wasn't. Oh, I'm nothing so gallant as a vampire-slayer, not me. Sorry if you hoped that was the next bit. No, I am just a nosy eighteen-year-old woman who sometimes— okay *often* (thank you, Dad)—takes herself a tad too seriously, and who *hates* to be beaten once she wakes up to a challenge. So, well . . . Reader, I *followed* him.

✷ↅ

Back on the glacial dance floor a thousand feet pounced, pranced, and stumbled, and the band played and the chandeliers shone.

And I slid like a panther, all right a *white* one, through the mob, spying on wicked Mr. Anghel whose second name no one seemed to know. (I had asked again, here and there, about him.)

First off he danced a waltz with a dazzled girl, who almost swooned and then was non-swooning and dis-dazzled when he abandoned her for another. (Later in the evening I came across knots of unsettled young women fuming or sighing or even sobbing—or plotting how to lure him back.)

He went through about ten girls in ten dances. He was picky, wasn't he? Of course, his partners, did they but know, were better off *not* being the selected maiden for the night's feast.

I did note he could dance stunningly well. Wondered briefly if he'd be as good in a club, decided he would be, as the vampire kind are simply wired to move well, in whatever context. It comes with the territory.

He never actually spotted *me*. I took care he didn't. I've said I'm pretty brilliant at seeming to be there when I'm not. I'm pretty good at doing the reverse too. But now and then he glanced around, looking for a split second slightly uneasy. He was A Vampire. He realized that *someone* was on his track. But I could see too he didn't truly reckon anyone was or could be. His madly *apparent* vampiricness was the camouflage. He was like an actor in the *rôle* of The Vampire. He *wants* to convince he is exactly that. The true vampire would cut his hair, dress in rags, and keep in the shadows.

All this anyhow, he center stage, me stalking unseen, went on for about two hours.

Then, *he found her*.

I was startled, and then less so. She was completely loud in clothes and make-up, with gold neon for hair. Quite pretty but mainly like a flag. The ideal choice. She thought she was the Star of the Night. She had convinced a lot of other people too that she was. Few therefore would doubt *he* thought so.

The target of some, by now, seventy-odd distracted jealousies, he drew her smoothly off the floor, and next they melted away onto another flight of watery stairs, and so down and out and in between the velvet curtains of the night.

&)CR

It was rather more challenging hunting them now, in all my white shimmer, for the dark was *dark* even if a half moon was rising on the lake. Yet here too, I could hide. A slant of moonlight through the shrubs, a blond deer slipping from tree to tree—a trick of the eyes.

That was me. (I'd better own up. Anthony taught me these skills, though I did have natural talent.)

He and she were fairly unoriginal in their choice of resting place, but then, I suppose, if you have a vast lake like a polished silver tray, and everywhere else the backdrop of darkness, you simply *have* to perch the edges of both. Which means, presumably, Anghel The Vampire was a romantic? He must have bought into his own legend in a big way.

I watched them a while, as they sat on a bench at the brim of the water. They talked, he speaking low and she . . . well, she had a kind of high and penetrating voice. "Oh, wow!" she kept saying, and, "What did you do then?" I could catch his words too—my hearing is fine—but they sounded like sort of movie dialogue. Quite *good* movie dialogue, but. He was telling her about his harsh life, and the novel he wanted to write, and sometimes he quoted a little poetry (Byron, Keats), and though when most guys do that they come over as truly useless, when he did it, it was quite impressive. But it was all a show, a sham. It was him being The Vampire, in the movie *rôle* he had invented, and for which he'd coined this well-written script.

I wondered if he even made himself sleep, by day, in some sort of *tomb*. If so, probably a really comfortable one, with a crystal goblet of bottled water on the side . . .

And then, quite abruptly, for somehow—even knowing it had to—I hadn't foreseen exactly when it would happen, he was bending toward her.

I thought, *Is she honestly so dumb she thinks this is just going to be a kiss?*

Sure. The idea of vampires *is* romantic. But not when you actually think about what they do. They bite you. Which, if that wasn't what you wanted, or expected, is an *assault* in anyone's book. And then—they steal your blood. Because again, unless you genuinely desire to nourish them in this way, it's *theft*. So what do those two procedures demonstrate a vampire to be? Shall I say: A mugger.

When he moved, so did I. I darted forward and burst out on them, white as vanilla ice cream. I made my voice even higher and more piercing than hers—which took some doing.

"Oh, hi! Am I *interrupting*? *Sorry!* But I'm just completely *lost*—and this is such a HUGE place, isn't it? Oh, do you mind if I sit down on your bench? I've been wandering around for over an hour. I mean, where *is* that castle? You wouldn't think, would you, you could lose a place that HUGE, but—" and down I flopped, with the sigh of a woman who just is not going to move for a while.

They were both gaping at me. She looked furious too. He, more as if he had just gotten the answer to a question that had been bothering him for hours. I had no doubt the answer was: *Yes! This plaster-of-Paris person is the one who was following me!*

I let a few moments pass, but neither she nor he spoke. Anyone else but the character I pretended to be would have grasped, however miles-thick they were, that *monsieur et mademoiselle* wished to be *left alone.*

Not I.

"What *ever* do you think of the ball?" I sparkled at them. "Isn't it too divine?"

"Then why," he said, in a low, dark, *awful* tone, "don't you go back to it?"

I'd tempted him from cover.

"I just said, you see," I replied, "I'm lost."

"I doubt that," he said. "If you walk up that path there, the path you just came down, I guess, you can see the house. You can't *miss* the house."

"Oh, really?" I gasped, and right then the neon girl clutched his arm, so for a second he scowled at her. She was in fact too thick herself to realize how terrible this scowl was. She said angrily, "Come on, Ang" (she pronounced that to rhyme with *hang*) "let's just get outta here."

And this was when the stag came shouldering from the woods about twenty feet away along the shore, noiseless and then *extremely* noisy, as branches went rushing and snapping out of the way of its great-antlered head, lit silver by the moonlight. Its eyes flashed electric green—and it bellowed.

That sound, from far off, had been devastating. Being close to it could cause total panic. I'd hoped so anyhow, when I was mentally coaxing the stag—that is, *one* of the stags—to come find us by the lake. This first-class animal had obliged. Neon spurted to her feet. Her eyes—her hair—had gone insane. She shrieked—and *ran*. She left us, him too, and bolted away, around the water and then off into the woods.

He, of course, didn't move.

Nor did I.

The stag though snorted down its gorgeous Roman nose, pawed the grass once as if to say, *You owe me, Lel,* then turned and sauntered back among the shadows.

He spoke once more.

"So you can do that too."

"Excuse me?"

He sighed deeply, stood up, and turned his elegant black velvet back to me. His black hair swung. "This is set in concrete then," he said. "You are to be my downfall."

"Er," I fluted, "my name's Lel."

"Let's not play games. I know you judged me at once, in the house. So, Lel. When do the heavies arrive?"

He had set his baleful eyes on me again. To my annoyance I found I wasn't ready for them. I should have been, shouldn't I. I wasn't a complete dope, like Neon.

"Why don't you sit down," I said.

"And let's talk it over? Very well."

But he stood there. Right next to me. I found too I was uncomfortably over-aware of him, but I should have been able to cope with

that, because I already *knew* the power he had, and in my case, prepared as I was, that power really could not and would not be having
an effect.

For quite a while then, we stayed, in silence.

The moon silvered the lake, shining it up like an old dollar.

Finally I glanced sidelong at him. He looked magnificently and
broodingly sad. Then, just sad. Like a child whose dog died, and he
never forgot, even ten years later, the way you *don't* ever forget the
ones you love. Things like that.

ജ◯രൂ

"Shall I tell you how I came to be—how I got like I am?"

This was what he eventually said. I'd already heard most of what I
took to be his "line." Obviously nothing to do with vampires, but
ancient feuds and some curse of his "ancestors" he hadn't believed. He
had been born on the borders of France, in a mountain region. His
family were aristocrats who had lost everything way back in the
1790s. He had escaped them, and now lived in one room, out here in
Chakhatti (the sticks), an impoverished writer who worked nights
waiting tables and pumping gas. But of course this mixture of Vampire
Angst and modern day necessity was all baloney (as Dad might say).

I hazarded a guess. "Your family is well off, something in big
business maybe. They live here and you were born here. You were
also well-educated, went to a top grade college—but left on discovering your true . . . how shall I say, vocation? Your family meanwhile
still support you financially, because you tell them you are teaching
yourself to be a writer."

He threw me a swift glare. "Not bad. Actually I received a
legacy—enough money to survive. That was from an aunt of mine.
They always thought she was crazy, but she was—what *I* am. She
was—"

"A vampire," I said.

"I have to assume," he said, flexing his hands (perhaps practicing how he would strangle me), "you don't believe vampires exist. That is, in the mythic sense. You just imagine I'm dangerous."

"Wrong again. I know true vampires are quite real. And I know, Mr. Anghel, you belong firmly among them."

"Usually people dismiss my *interests* as . . . a fantasy."

I gazed hard at the lake. He was much too distracting.

"The only thing that's a fantasy here," I answered, pleased at my own crisp tone, "is your total misunderstanding of what *being* a vampire entails."

"Some secret society—a code known only to the few—" he solemnly said.

"No. Frankly, the opposite," He had turned and I felt him stare at me. It was compelling but I didn't allow myself to react. To the lake alone I added, "You need to talk to someone. If you're as messed up as I think you are, you need some *help*."

He gave a bitter, quite violent laugh.

"Sure. You mean a shrink."

"You need," I continued, "to speak to my father."

"Your—your *what*?"

"Father." I opened the tiny white glitzy evening purse I'd been given, and pulled out one of Anthony's cards, and handed it to him.

He stared at that, now.

"This is some joke, right?"

"No joke, Mr. Anghel—"

"Will you quit that *Mister* stuff—how fucking old do you think I am?"

"You could be a thousand. But no joke. This is for real. If you prefer, I can start you off on the road to redemption by just asking you nine straight questions. All *you* need do is reply, and be honest."

Finally our eyes met.

I thought—well. I thought in one big golden blank. To my relief my voice came out again, not in a husky squeak, but crisp now as very dry toast. I was at my most business-like, and that was how I asked those nine questions.

ဆာ

"First question: Do you reflect in mirrors or reflective surfaces?"

"I don't look anymore. Obviously I don't. I'm undead. My soul—or whatever—that's gone. So, no reflection. The night I realized I threw any mirrors away. And yes, I've learned to shave by touch. I'm good at that, dexterous. It seems to be part of what I am, what I can do, now. The same as I can seem to vanish, even on an empty side-walk . . . that kind of thing."

"Okay. Second question. Do you go out by day?"

"*You are kidding me.* What do *you* think? Do I look like a case from a burns unit? Yeah, I did once make a mistake. Last winter. I was walking around in broad daylight for one half hour. I was blistered so bad, even inside my clothes, I had to hide for three nights. My *skin*, bits of it, fell off in patches. No. I *don't* go out in sunlight. Sunset is dawn for my kind."

"Question three: How old *are* you?"

"Twenty-two this fall. Next week in fact. I suppose I'll live forever, but I only got started on this *thing* about sixteen months ago."

"Question four—"

"Wait a minute—"

"Question four—" I paused, but he didn't interrupt again. Just looked. With his sorrowful dark eyes. "Do you take and drink human blood? Is that your food?"

"Yes. You know that already. That was what you broke up back there. Me, trying to take and drink and feed on *blood*."

"Question five." (He sighed. Nothing else.) "Do you otherwise eat and drink?"

"No. Oh, water's okay—a glass of wine. Even a beer or a coke. Fluids seem to digest. I don't risk anything else."

"So your last meal was—"

"Sixteen months ago. I threw it right up."

"So blood is your only sustenance. Which leads us to question six: How often do you do this?"

"Once a week. Roughly. I can go a month without, if I have to. But if I don't it's—all I can think of."

"Rather like partying with a so-called recreational drug, yes?"

"I wouldn't know," he said icily. "I never tried those."

"Fine. Question seven: Do you shape-shift? I mean, can you seem to become another thing, an animal say, or even an inanimate object?"

"Yes." (He sounded almost embarrassed, as if he boasted and hadn't wanted to.) "A wolf. Mostly. But once I—I kind of made myself kind of like a phone booth."

I couldn't help it. I burst out laughing. "Did anyone try to—get inside and *make a call?*"

He grinned.

Oh. The grin was beautiful too.

"Yeah. But the door stayed shut."

I pulled us back to grim reality.

"Question eight: Ever killed anyone, Anghel?"

"My God—no. *No.* I don't—I'm careful. It's bad enough being— what I am. I don't want to be a murderer as well."

We were both standing up now. I wasn't sure when I did.

I said, "Question nine, then. And this is the last one. How did you find out you'd become a vampire?"

"How did I—? Look, I'd had suspicions before that we—my family—had the gene for it. I suppose it *is* a gene. Like some families having the gene for red hair, or a particular allergy. . . . I know how it is in books, movies. Someone does it to you, takes your blood and makes you a vampire, just like they are. It didn't happen that way. I said my aunt—I came to realize she was—she was a vampire. She'd just seemed to think she was mad. Everybody put everything weird about her down to that—avoiding sunlight, not eating, that stuff. By the time I connected it all up, she'd been dead two years. And she had left me the legacy. Like she knew I would be the same. So I put it together. I still didn't believe it at first. I said, I want—*wanted* to be a writer. So I started to *write* about it, about my life if I had been, if I *was*, a vampire. I was trying to sort it out.

"Then I met a girl at some party in Manhattan. And she'd read a story of mine, a pretty lurid one, in some magazine and she—she wanted to act it out with me. Scared me. But when I'm scared—then sometimes I have to do it. Prove to myself I can. So, we did. I didn't hurt her. It's important to me you understand that. She loved every minute, and I had a real difficult time putting her off after. But for me—something changed. Something changed when I took the blood. It was—" he hesitated, looking out at the lake and the moon—"it was like finding something in your own self, *meeting* who you really are—and I wasn't who I'd ever thought. And I was—not better—but I *fit*. And when I went out of the apartment, everything—the street, the city . . . it was *alive*, and I was *alive*, in a way it and I had never been, not until then. Do you begin to see? I can't explain it. I can write with words, use them, make them work. But with this, I can't *find* the words. It was like I'd walked out—not of a room, but of a dark *cave*. My whole world had only *been* a cave—but now the lights were on and the true world was there all around me, and inside me, forever.

"So I've answered all your questions, and now I guess your wonderful father and his men arrive and finish me off. Right, Lel? That name on the card though, that's a lie, isn't it? Only one thing puzzles me. Shouldn't it read 'Anthony *Van Helsing*'?"

I shook my head. "*Oh* no, it surely should not. That name on the card is a family name. It's mine too."

He looked quizzical. Sad and quizzical and courageous, all ready to meet some horrible bloodthirsty anti-vampire end of sharpened stakes and villagers with flaming torches ready to burn him alive.

It must have been that that made me feel protective, and want to put my arms around him.

But anyhow that was when he laughed again, a very different silky, inky laugh—and then he was gone. There instead stood a great black wolf, the height of a mastiff dog, with eyes like rubies. The wolf too seemed to be laughing. But the next second it sprang away, and dove along the lake shore and into the trees.

And *my* next move? I stood there cursing myself.

I knew he wasn't headed for the house, or the town. He had vanished not only from his human shape but out of the life of anyone who'd recently known him. Though everything he said, I was certain, was honest and true, with my artful, smug little plans I'd cornered him, and blown the whole thing. I'd lost him. And worse than that, I had lost him also his own chance of living free and safe in this mad world he had only properly come to see sixteen months before. Oh, Lel. Clever, cunning, know-it-all, stupid, dumb damn Lel.

❧☙

My father is a physician. He deals with sickness of the psyche and the mind. He has endlessly various patients. He is *good*.

He went into this line of work, as he would be the first to say, because he had already cured both himself, and another member of his family, of a pretty dire life-destructive mental illness. His name, which is real enough, is quite a talking point, but he's found, as I have on the whole, it causes startled amusement rather than giving anything away. It's like that thing about camouflage I mentioned earlier.

Vampirism isn't a disease. It isn't a possession or an evil spell or the devil's work. *It's a way of evolving.* Because the human race did and does evolve. Superman, Batman—they're already around out there. If they keep a low profile, do you *blame* them? A vampire, or what's come to be called a vampire (the word seems to come from ancient Turkey, and means something like *magician*), is just one more variety of this evolving super-race, the one we watch on screen and read about in books, but which most of us seldom think may just have sat there next to us on the subway.

Vampires are this: They grow up but stay young for a very long while (centuries sometimes). They don't need food or drink, though they *can* eat and drink a little, if they want. Taking another person's blood can bring out awareness of themselves and what they are. But that is only because they have already bought into the idea. That is, they *think* it will, so it does. And in fact where they can come to awareness of the truth *without* assault and robbery, they come to it better and more fully, and with far less damage to themselves. Put it this way: They only go after that blood because they have the notion they are, on some level, vampires. So taking the blood isn't needed. What *is* needed is just facing up to the facts.

Feeding on or drinking blood is—*redundant*. People are *not* the allotted prey, and blood is *not* the essential food. *No vampire on Earth has to have blood.* Just as they don't have to have ordinary food or fluid either. So the Blood Feast made so popular in stories only has value (if that is the right word) in sometimes shocking them into focus for themselves. And believe me, it also hurts them on some deep level too. If you aren't a vampire, though, grabbing blood won't do a darn thing for you. I mean you won't be able to shape-shift or apparently disappear, let alone live to three hundred and forty-nine. Oh, and no vampire can turn anyone else into one by taking their blood. Unless, of course, they already *were* one to start with.

So, the meaning of blood for vampires is basically a misunderstanding. It has nothing to do with drink or food, with goblets and dishes and the dining table of the world. It is blood*lines*—it's *genes*—as Anghel said. And if you've gotten that gene, you have it. You are a vampire, a Being of the Blood. And one day you'll wake up, and *know*, even if it takes till you're fifty and you look in a mirror (yes, I did say mirror) and think—*I only look twenty-two still. How can this be?*

Because vampires *do* reflect in mirrors, in all reflective surfaces. They cast shadows too. They can even go out all day long in the blazing summer sun. No tan, sure. But the sun won't fry you. Unless, of course, brainwashed by hundreds of years of legendary propaganda, you *believe it will.*

You see, all that stuff is a psychosomatic illness. It *seems* real, so real you'll have the symptoms, as can happen with any major psychosomatic sickness. And in fact a vampire's own abilities can turn against him to reinforce the myth. A vampire *can* seem invisible—so in that looking glass, he *is*. So you come up in blisters too, and seek a big box to sleep in, and hunt down innocent people and mug them for blood. You can even throw up at the smell of garlic, or pass out at a powerful religious symbol. But it isn't for real. It is a kind of *guilt trip*. The vampire knows he is superior. That frightens him. So, unconsciously, he tries to keep himself chained up. No one can be harder on us than we are ourselves, once we've gotten started.

Otherwise, a vampire can live forever, maybe. But you don't need a stake or fire to kill him. You can just shoot a vampire dead, and you won't need a special bullet. Vampires are long-lived, not invulnerable. What they can also do are things like seem to be other creatures, vanish, sometimes fly, and, obviously, call animals to them and ask *them* to do things—like a stag, for example. We don't abuse these gifts. Not when we grasp what we are and why. But then, some of us are lucky. I grew up in a partly vampiric family. I knew by age three what I was, and when I found on my tenth birthday I could turn into a fox, my Dad took a photo of me like that. I still have that picture. Yes, cameras can catch us too.

My father does look remarkably young. He puts it down, to his patients, as the vitamins he takes. And his name—our family name?

Draculian. Anthony Draculian. Lelystra Draculian. But no, we're not from that famous branch of our kind (the Romanian one, brought to public attention in the 1800s by clever Mr. Stoker). Though, if you trace bloodlines back far enough, we are related.

And there, you see, these were all the things I should have said to poor handsome unhappy Anghel. And instead I'd been flustered and messed up.

∞∞

I had to stay another two days with the Kokersons. I did it and it was hell. But then, there wasn't much point in running back to Dad two days early, howling about my dismal failure. Anghel was gone. I knew I'd never see him again, I knew I could have helped and instead I only helped make his life worse.

I did put one call through to Dad. But he was with a patient. Oh, let it wait then till I was home. I'd have all the rest of my days after all, to blame myself, and to regret.

∞∞

Anthony has his office way across town. We live in a big russet brownstone on the corner of Dale and Landry. It's a nice area.

I'd tried to call him again from the cell phone booth on the train, but he was back in another eternal meeting. No one was home.

I dumped my bags and then took the little elevator up to our roof garden. It's only a little garden, a kind of outdoor living room. The last roses were dying on the walls, but the grapevine had big purple grapes. I took some off and ate them, gazing down over the parapet at the sun deciding to sink, as it always does, west of the city.

I had never felt I had to go rob someone of their blood. Lucky in that, I said. Lucky me. I'd had it all very easy. Only when Mom died—I was fifteen then. That had been hard. She wasn't like us, Dad and me, or my uncle. She didn't have the gene. I knew they'd talked about—when she was older, how they would handle that. . . . But it never happened, a truck in town saw to that. It killed her. And we, Dad and me, we wouldn't be immune to that either.

The sky was rose-gold. Birds were flying like scribbles over it. The city made its noises of trains and cabs and people, but I knew the moment my father came back in the house I would sense it, I always did. And then the oddest idea went through my mind. It made me straighten up and hold my breath a moment. This strange thought was—had my father, my clever amazing father who seemed always to know everything—had he known too Anghel was due to be at the Kokerson's weird ball. Had he known I would see what Anghel was—might try to alter things—even think I'd be the one to save Anghel from the dark he'd stumbled into? If that was it, how much more awful it was going to be, telling Anthony that I *hadn't*—

And this was when I picked up what must *be* Dad, that silent step of his I can always hear, just inside the door below. And next the elevator rising.

I was horrified. Not of Dad—of the thing I'd have to say. I braced myself, with the taste of the grapes in my mouth. And out onto the roof he walked. But it wasn't Anthony. It was Anghel.

I froze. Like the biggest fool (the one who wins the Oscar for idiocy), I said, "Whuh?"

And he grinned.

His hair was tied back, a long, long black tail falling down his back. He wore jeans, a shirt, a light leather jacket. Even this way, as I had predicted, you couldn't miss he was something else. Different, astonishing.

He said, "It's okay, Lel. I have a pass for the door. Your father gave it to me. He trusts me. Can you?"

Anthony only ever trusts those who really can be trusted.

But I'd been kidding myself, hadn't I? It wasn't just I felt I'd messed up, let Anghel, a *patient*, down. It was me I was unhappy for. I hadn't been able to stop thinking of him. I thought I had lost him for good. But here he was.

Very coolly I said, "It's early for you to be out, isn't it? I mean, the sun's not down yet, is it."

"He said—Anthony said—take it slow, but try a few new things. So, I do. Just an hour after sunrise, an hour before sunset. And look—" he was close now, holding out his strong, elegant hands. "Not a single burn."

I swallowed. "So you *are* my father's patient."

"Since yesterday. I've made great strides, yes?"

"Yes. Good." Lamely I studied the buttons on his shirt. They were fine, for buttons. It was better than looking up into his eyes.

"Lel," he said quietly, "thank you."

So then I had to look. When I did, those hands reached out and gently took mine. His touch was fiery, but what else? Something in his eyes had altered too. They weren't less overpowering exactly, but—there was something else in them now. I could see—*Anghel.* That is, I think I mean I could see who he truly was. A man not cruel or mean or a robber, never stupid, rich in possibility, brave, yes, *gallant*—only wanting to find his way.

"I apologize for the wolf stuff—the shape-shift," he said to me. "I was—confused. Had to sort it out. As you see, though, I didn't lose the card. And I called Anthony, and I saw him yesterday. He's okay, your father."

"Yes, he is."

He still held my hands. "Lel," he said, and then, very softly, "Lelystra—" And for the first time in my entire life my name sounded wonderful to me, as if I'd never *heard* it before—"Lelystra, you saved my skin. You saved my sanity. You stopped me becoming something I'd never want. And I don't want—I can't make you any promises, or ask for any. Not yet. Not until I *know* I'm really *there*, where I have to be. Where *you* are. But if I make it, then—"

The whole roof was glowing now, the walls, the vines, the grapes, blood-red from the sunfall. And in the blood-red light Anghel leaned forward and kissed my mouth. It was a marvelous kiss, weightless yet profound. As gently as he, I gave it back to him. There in the sunset light as red as blood.

Changed

Nancy Holder

*T*he vampires invaded New York the night Jilly turned sixteen. She was pacing in front of a club called Watami, waiting for Eli to show, eager to see what he had bought her. He was late, and she knew it was Sean's fault. Sean wouldn't want to come, because it was Jilly's birthday and Sean hated her. But Eli would make him do it, and they would show and she would wonder all over again why Eli couldn't love her like that . . . and how he could love someone who didn't like her.

Then, out of nowhere, the place was swarming with white-faced, bone-haired, blood-eyed monsters. They just started *attacking*, grabbing people and ripping open their throats—dancers, drinkers, bartenders, and her three best straight friends, Torrance, Miles, and Diego.

She still had no idea how she'd gotten out of there, but she called Eli first and then her parents. *No service, no service, beepbeepbeep* . . . no texting, no net; no one could freakin' communicate.

She was Jilly Stepanek, lately of the Bronx, a semi-slacker who wanted to go to film school at NYU once she got her grades back up. She had been a neo-goth, into Victorian/Edwardian clothes and pale makeup without the Marilyn Manson vibe, loved steampunk—but now all she was, was another terrified chick on the run from the monsters. Used to be the monsters were in her head; now they were breathing down her neck in real time.

No one stepped forward to represent the vampires or explain why they had taken over the five boroughs like the world's worst gang. There were no demands, no negotiations, just lots of dying. In less than a week, drained corpses—the homeless, first—littered the streets of Manhattan, SoHo, and the Village. As far as Jilly could tell, none of them rose to become vampires themselves. Maybe all the movies weren't true; maybe once they killed you, you were just dead.

The vampires had hunting animals like falcons that dug into their white arms. They were all head and wings, with huge white faces and bloodshot eyes and teeth that clack-clack-clacked like the windup false kind. Blood dripped and splattered onto the ground from the places the bird-suckers gouged their claws into their masters' arms, but—she observed from as far away as possible—either the vampires couldn't feel it or they liked it. Maybe it was their version of cutting.

The bird-suckers swooped and pirouetted across the night clouds, tearing the city pigeons to pieces. A few nights of slaughter and they owned the skies. A few nights more, and there were no wild dogs on the island of Manhattan.

Three nights after her birthday, a vampire attacked and killed her father; its vampire-bird ran her mother to the ground while they were running out of their house. Jilly screamed for her mom to run faster, run faster, oh, God, but it swooped down on the back of her mother's head and started pecking and tearing. Her mother fell; her eyes were open but she wasn't seeing a thing. Blood from her neck gushed onto the sidewalk beneath a lamp post, and it looked like her shadow was seeping out of her body.

Hiding in the bushes, heaving, Jilly waited it out. Then she ran the other way, in nothing but a black chemise, some petticoats, her boots, and a long black coat she had bought at a garage sale.

She tried to get to Eli's row house but whole blocks exploded right in front of her, and others whooshed up in flames like paper lanterns. Weeping and gasping, she phoned him over and over; she texted with shaking hands. *No service, no service, beepbeepbeep.*

She raced in circles to get past the fires as the smoke boiled up into the dotted clouds of clack-clack-clacking birds.

By four days after her birthday, the streets were a real jungle. The survivors were as vicious as the street dogs the vampires-birds had eaten: hoarding food, and threatening to kill each other over safe places to sleep and water bottles. She had some experience with hostility, from when she had gone drug-mad. Rehab and a lot of love had redeemed her, but the old lessons were not forgotten.

Dodging fiends and madmen, she stole tons of phones—or maybe she only took them, since there was no one left alive in the stores to ring up the sales—but there was really, really, really no service. Trying to find one that worked became an addiction. At least it gave her something to do—other than hide, and run.

Her therapist, Dr. Robles, used to caution her to ease up, not use her busy brain quite so much. He said she had to let go of loving Eli because people who were gay were gay; there wasn't going to be a change of heart no matter how much she wanted one.

She tried to find a cybercafé that the vampires hadn't gutted, but there were none to be found. She broke into office buildings and tried their computers, but they were fried. She wondered how the vampires did it. She was sure it was part of their plot to take over the world.

Just like the vampires, she slept during the day, in the brightest sunlight she could find, her black coat covering her like a shroud. Even though she had never been a Catholic, she prayed to the God of the crucifix, because crucifixes could hold the vampires at bay. She wanted to pray in St. Patrick's Cathedral but it was too dark and enclosed; she could almost hear the vampires hissing in the chapels lining the sanctuary. Her lips were cracked and chapped. She was filthy. But maybe God would help her anyway.

Please, God, please, God, please, God, please, God, please please please don't let Eli get burned to death or sucked dry by the demons amen.

High rises burned down to ash; cars exploded, and the vampires capered on stacks of the dead. And Jilly staggered through it like the last victim of the Apocalypse. No one hooked up with her and she didn't make any effort to take on a sidekick or become one. She had to get to Eli; at least she could die with him.

So she kept skirting the crazily burning buildings in her tattered bad-fairy gear, the indigo in her hair bleached by the sun and coated with dirt. She showed people the photograph of him she always carried in her coat pocket. *No, Jilly, no, Jilly, no, Jilly, no Jilly, no Jilly, no no no sorry, loser.*

She kept waiting for the fires to burn down, burn out. The smoke took a toll on her; the air smelled like someone barbecuing rotten hot dogs; she felt it congealing in her lungs and coating her skin. Five days after her birthday, she was so tired she could hardly breathe anyway, which was a sort of blessing because maybe she would die and then she could stop everything. Escaping the bad was also one of her habits. She was empty, outside and in, just a husk. If a vampire tried to suck her blood, it would probably find nothing but red powder.

She really thought that the time had come for her to die. She thought about her parents, and her friends, but mostly she thought about Eli Stein. He had been her first and only love, before he had realized he was gay. She still loved him; she would always love him, no matter what form his love for her would take. *Brainbrain, go away, obsess again some other day. . . .*

He was crazy-mad for Sean instead and she hoped. . . .

No, she couldn't even think that. If she went anywhere near praying for something to happen to Sean. . . .

You are evil, Jilly, and you deserve to die.

Beneath her coat, she fell asleep and dreamed of Eli, and Sean; because in the summer after tenth grade that was who they were, Eliandsean, like one person, like the person she had hoped to become with him. Once Eli had found his other half, they had come to her house almost every day, because they could hold hands there.

They could brag about their slammin' skillz on their skateboards and video games like any other teenage boys, and they could flirt with each other and sit on the couch with their arms around each other while Jilly's mom brought them sodas and grilled cheese sandwiches. They were amazed and delighted by the acceptance in Jilly's house. Tolerance, in her house, came after a hard struggle, won by determined parents who never let go of Jilly, even after she ran away with a biker, shaved her head, and told her shrink there were no bones in her hands.

It was all crazy in a new way; taggers wrote VAMPIRES SUCK over every surface there was, and people tried to share whatever information they'd learned about them: They were mindless, they were super smart; they had a leader, it was all random. They lured you in with dark sexuality. They attacked you like animals without a plan. It had something to do with global warming; they were terrorists. They were a plague created by the government.

She saw plenty of them. White-faced and leering, they darted down streets and stared out of windows, like terrible Will Smith CGI effects. She didn't know how she hadn't been killed yet, with all the near misses. One thing she did know, they were more like people than beasts. Just very evil people. Their birds were mindless attackers, but the vampires themselves listened to music and went joyriding on motorcycles and kept the subway people alive so they could go on rides; *it's a dead world after all.*

After another near miss—a vampire turned a corner just ahead of her, and she turned on her heel and ran, hard—she broke down weeping, her thin stomach contracting; and then God must have taken the hint, or felt guilty, or whatever, but He/She/It/They did something miraculous:

It began to rain. Hard. Buckets poured down from heaven like old lady angels washing their doorstoops; gallons and rivers tumbled onto rooftops and treetops like all the tears of all the New Yorkers, like all the blood that had gushed out of the necks of the dead.

And the rain toned down the fires just enough that she soaked her coat and then raced through the fire line, arriving on the other side into some kind of hellish otherworld; everything was covered with gray and white-bone ash: trees, buildings, abandoned cars, rubble. She shuffled through layers of powdery death.

And there it was. *There it was.*

Eli's row house. With the formerly turquoise paint and the American flags and some kid's ash-colored tricycle overturned in a pile of ash like strange granular leaves. Then she thought she saw a shadow move across the window, and she stared at it for a long time, because she had actually made it, and in her heart she'd expected there to be no signs of life. There were no more shadows and she wondered if she had gone crazy or died and imagined the whole thing. By then, Jilly was certain the dead could be as crazy as the living. She staggered up the stoop stairs, kicking up layers of death that made her gag and choke.

She knocked on the door, but no one answered, and she pushed it open.

Eli and his father faced each other in the living room with the old tapestry of the Jews at Masada hanging over the upright piano. Eli looked taller and thinner, his dark hair long as ever, and he had a semi-beard. He looked like a leftist rabbi in the NYU sweatshirt she had given him. Mr. Stein was still Mr. Stein, in a navy blue sweater and dark trousers.

Mr. Stein was shouting. "You stupid faggot, you're going to die out there."

"Just shut up!" Eli shrieked. "Stop calling me that!"

"Eli," she whispered from the doorway. "Eli, it's me."

They both turned.

"Jilly!"

Eli whooped, gathered her up, and hugged her against himself. She felt as light as a desiccated leaf, unbelievably dizzy, and reeling with happiness. Eli was alive. He was safe. And he was still here, in his old house, living indoors, with his parents.

"Oh, my God, are you okay?" he asked; and then, before she could answer, he said, "Have you seen Sean?"

"No," she said, and he deflated. She saw the misery on his face, felt it in the way he nearly crushed her.

In the kitchen, his gaunt, black-haired witchmother was *cooking*, as if nothing had changed. They had electricity, and gas, and as Jilly smelled the hot food—onions, meat—her mouth began to salivate. She burst into tears and he held her tightly, swaddling her in himself. He smelled so good. So clean. Almost virginal.

His father's eyes bulged like an insect's and he stared at Jilly, as if she were an intruder.

"I've been trying to get here," she said. "Everything was on fire. And then the rain came."

"The rain," Mr. Stein said reverently, glancing at the tapestry.

"Now we can look for Sean." Eli said.

"Don't speak that name." Mr. Stein snapped.

For God's sake, what do you care about that now? she wanted to snap back at him. But she took Eli's hand and folded it under her chin. She saw the layer of ash-mud on her hands and wondered what she looked like. A zombie, probably.

"I was just about to leave, to search for him," he said, bringing her knuckles to his mouth. He kissed them, then laid her hand against his cheek. His tears dampened her skin, like more rain. "He called just before it happened, from midtown. I don't know what he was doing there. We had a fight. I was lying down."

Weren't you going to meet me at the club?

Eli searched Jilly's face with his fingers and she felt each brush of his fingertips close a wound the long days and nights had cut into her soul. There was no one she loved more. She would go to her grave loving Eli Stein.

"Of course you're not leaving now. Look at her. She looks like she's dead." Mr. Stein had never liked her. Not only was she formerly a mad slut, she wasn't Jewish, and her family had given Eli and Sean safe harbor to commit their carnal atrocities.

"You need to fix the door," Jilly said. "Or at least to lock it."

"I thought it was locked," Mr. Stein said. He looked at Eli. "Did you unlock it?" He walked to the door to check it, passing close by Jilly so that she had to take a step out of his way. He grabbed the door; she heard a click, and then he turned the knob.

"It's broken." He glared at Eli. "Did you break it?"

"Dad, why would I do that?" Eli asked.

"Maybe vampires tried to get in last night," Jilly ventured. "You need to put up some crucifixes. They really do work."

Mr. Stein crossed his arms over his chest. "Not normal," he muttered.

"Dinner is almost ready," Mrs. Stein announced from the kitchen, smiling weakly. Jilly wondered where on Earth she had found a brisket. In the still-working refrigerator of their house, she supposed.

Eli gave her a look that said, *My parents have lost their minds, obviously.* He had some experience with mental illness, since he was her best friend.

She didn't smile, even though, as usual, they were thinking the same thing. It wasn't funny. She didn't know who was crazy and who wasn't.

"You could take a shower, Jilly," Mrs. Stein continued.

Jilly was too weak and exhausted to take a shower. But Mrs. Stein gave her some mashed potatoes and a piece of cheese and they energized her enough to stagger into the bathroom. For the first time in weeks, she was a few degrees less afraid to be enclosed in a small room; to take off her clothes; to stand vulnerable underneath water . . .

. . . and then Eli was in the bathroom, taking off his clothes too. He climbed into the shower and wrapped his arms around her, sobbing. She started to cry, too, naked with her best friend who did not want her the way she wanted him; they clung to each other and mourned.

"He's out there," he said. "I know he is."

She turned around and leaned her back against his chest. It was so unreal that she was here. To just walk through their door . . .

"Your parents are probably out there having a fit," she said, her eyes closed as she savored the pleasure of mist, and warmth, and Eli.

"Are you crazy? They're probably dancing in circles. 'He's in there with a girl! He's not gay! He's not a faggot!'" He mimicked his father's voice perfectly. Then he added softly, "What about your parents?"

She raised her chin so the water would sluice over her face. Her silence was all he needed.

"Oh, Jilly. Jilly, God, what happened?"

"I can't talk about it. Don't say anything. I'll never stop crying."

He laid his hand over her forehead. "I'll only say that they were so good to me. And in Judaism, goodness is a living thing," he whispered.

"Thanks." She licked her stinging lips again.

Head dipped, he turned off the water. Then he toweled her off and retrieved some neatly folded clothes set out by his mother in the hall. A pair of sweat pants swam on her and belled around her ankles. There was a black sweater, no bra. Not that it mattered.

He put back on his clothes, laced his fingers with hers, and took her into his room. There were pictures of her everywhere—at school, at their first Broadway play, holding hands in Central Park. The ones of Sean outnumbered them, though. First there were a lot of pictures of just the two of them, Eli and Sean, the brand-new boyfriends; and then, of Eli, Sean, *and* Jilly, as Eli brought the two "together"—mugging for the camera, practicing for a drama skit, their very silly trip to a book signing at Forbidden Planet. Sean looked pissed off in any picture she was in. Didn't Eli notice?

She stretched out on the blue velour bedspread, feeling as if she had just set down a heavy load of books. It was incredible to her that he had been sleeping on this wonderful bed, in his own room. She didn't even know if her building was still standing. She could go back, get more clothes, get her valuables and money.

Eli would go with her. They could look for Sean on the way.

She dozed. Eli spooned her, holding her; each time she inhaled, he exhaled. It had been that way in the early days, for them. When Sean came along, he added something new; he was a literal breath of fresh air. Even Jilly had been charmed by the surfer dude who had lived in L.A. and knew movie people who might be able to help her. He talked about working as a stand-in. He hung around stunt men. His uncle had rented out his surf shop as a movie set.

But once he was sure of Eli's love, he changed. She saw it happen. Eli didn't. Maybe changed was the wrong word; around her, he became chilly and disinterested, and she knew he was never going to introduce her to anyone in the industry. But Eli didn't see it.

Sean had actually been a kind of vampire. He sucked up anything he wanted; he drained Eli's friends and classmates by using them to advance up the social ladder, then blindsided them with his snotty I-am-mean-and-because-I-deserve-to-be-you-must-permit-it attitude. She could almost predict when he'd show his other face. Jilly's mom used to say they should give Sean the benefit of the doubt because he had been through a lot. Any guy who was gay had suffered. So they had to be nice to him, even though he was a jerk. She knew what her mom was not saying: *We put up with your bad behavior. Welcome to the real world—the one that does not revolve around you.*

Her mom would never say anything like that, of course.

Because she was dead.

But she had never talked like that, not even when Jilly was the most drug-crazy; she had said Jilly was hurting.

But even when Jilly was at her worst, she still would have done anything to help Eli become more, and more, and more of all the wonderful things Eli was.

"God, I'm glad you're here," he whispered, nuzzling the back of her head. She cried some more, and he held her.

There was a soft knock on the door. Mrs. Stein whispered, "It's dinner time."

Jilly was very hungry, and the smell of food was making her clench and unclench her hands. But Eli had fallen asleep with his arm over her. She tried to figure out a way to slide out from underneath him without waking him up. She couldn't manage it, so she stayed beside him. Her arm began to ache. Her stomach growled.

As she contracted and released her muscles, trying to keep the blood circulating, she heard Mrs. Stein crying. It was a high-pitched, irritating kind of weeping, and it set Jilly on edge.

"No one is helping us!" Mrs. Stein cried. "No one."

Jilly, hungry and despairing and exhausted, listened to the rain, and imagined New York City going up in steam. Then she let herself go fully to sleep for the first time since she had turned sixteen.

∞∞∞

The yelling jerked Jilly awake.

"You will die!" Mr. Stein shouted downstairs.

"Stop yelling!" Mrs. Stein was crying again. "You'll drive him away, the way you always have."

"What, drive away? Didn't you hear what he just said? He's leaving anyway!"

Jilly groaned, feeling in the bed for Eli, realizing he'd gotten up. His parents were trying, in their way, to tell him that they loved him and didn't want him to risk his life by leaving their home. She felt the same way. She didn't want to get out of bed. She knew Eli so well, knew they were going to leave as soon as she emerged from the bedroom—*maybe we can eat first*—and it wasn't going to be a graceful exit.

∞

"It's because they blame you for not fixing me," Eli told her as they left his parents' house. It was still raining; Mrs. Stein had given them parkas with hoods and umbrellas. The rain seemed to have cleared the sky of the vampire birds of prey. Another miracle.

At least they had gotten to have some breakfast first—last night's brisket, and pancakes. And blessed coffee. While she'd been on the street, she'd heard a story that one man had knifed another over the last cup of coffee in a pot in a diner.

She didn't say anything. She couldn't forgive Eli's parents for being so narrow-minded as to pick a fight with their son and his best friend, when they might never see either of them alive again.

She adjusted the heavy backpack, filled with extra clothes, shampoo, toothbrushes, and toothpaste. Eli was carrying the heavier one, packed with food. He had a small satchel over his shoulder too, packed with photographs of Sean, seven of them, as if someone might not recognize him in the first six. Sean was weird-looking, with almond-shaped eyes and a long, hooked nose in a long, narrow face. So he wasn't handsome, he wasn't nice, and there were other gay guys in their school if Eli wanted a boyfriend. Gay guys who liked Jilly a lot. Unfortunately, Sean was the guy for him.

Eli groaned when they reached the pocket park, site of their first make-out session, after her birthday party in the eighth grade. She'd been so excited and happy she hadn't slept all night.

"Even the trees got burned up," he said. They walked close together, holding hands. She had a strange floating sensation; if he hadn't held on to her, she thought she might have floated away from sheer fear.

They passed dozens of burning buildings, sizzling and steaming in the rain. The subway station split the sidewalk; by mutual unspoken consent, they gave it a wide berth. Darkness and seclusion— perfect vampire territory.

Shadows and shapes moved in the alleyways; they walked down the center of the street, gripping each other's hand. It was strange, but Jilly was more afraid with Eli there than she had been by herself. She didn't think she could stand it if something happened to him. He was so nervous; he was broadcasting "come and get me" to anyone interested in easy pickings.

He pulled a cell phone out of his parka and dialed numbers, listening each time. Finally he grunted and put it back in his pocket, and moved his bangs out of his eyes. Her heart stirred, and she touched his cheek. He smiled distractedly; she knew he was glad she was there, but it was Sean he most wanted to see.

She used to have these long conversations with her girl friends about if Eli would ever come back to her. Eli had been her actual boyfriend for two years. They had made out all the time, but never gone any farther than that. They'd been too young. Then he and Sean had found each other . . . or rather, Sean had found him. Sean had moved to New York and zeroed in on Eli, even before Sean was sure Eli was gay. So Eli had given Jilly the "we can still be friends" speech.

Only in their case, it was true. They were excellent friends. They thought alike, read alike. He thought NYU was a great goal. He talked about going there too. They both hated sports. And Sean, who was a jock, hated that.

He never said a word about it to Eli. As far as Eli was concerned, Sean loved Jilly like a sister. Had used those exact words, in fact, the one time Jilly tried to discuss it with him. But when Eli wasn't paying attention, Sean zinged her out with vast amounts of passive-aggressive

BS—veiled threats and lots of snark. He picked fights just before they were supposed to meet her somewhere—like Watami. Being somewhere in midtown when he was supposed to celebrate with her was classic Sean, King of Bitter Homosexuality.

Eli brushed it off, refused to agree to her reality. So she didn't bring it up again, ever. She didn't want to give Sean the ammunition for an "It's either her or me" speech.

As they walked out of the burn zone, the sky began to darken, and a rush of resentment roared through Jilly. Her tired body was aching for Eli's soft, clean bed. She wanted to take another shower, and brush her teeth for a year. She didn't want to be risking her life, or Eli's, for someone who hated her.

Her mind was trying to figure out what life would be like if they found Sean. And then, before she knew what she was doing, she said, "Watami. The club. Maybe he went there."

He looked at her. "He wasn't going to go. And he'd come to my house first, or try to get to me through our friends." And they did have other friends, gay friends, who envied them for having Jilly's family to hang with.

"Okay, never mind. Maybe he went to school."

Eli raised his brows. "Maybe." He smiled. "It's big. Maybe they're doing like a Red Cross shelter there." He hugged her. "You're a genius, Jilly."

Too smart for my own good, she thought. The old Jilly, pre-rehab—the one without the boundaries—might not have suggested places to look for Sean. But Jilly was a good, nice person now. Maybe that was why he didn't love her. She wasn't edgy enough. She could change. . . .

But he can't. He is gay, she reminded herself.

It was nearly dark. It was so dangerous to be out like this; she'd seen vampires leap from the shadows and drag people away. Sometimes they growled; sometimes they were silent. Jilly had been sleeping next to an old lady in a store one night. In the morning, all that was left of the lady were her shoes. Jilly had no idea why she herself had been left alive. Maybe the old lady had been enough.

They met a man on the street a few blocks from the school named Bo. He staggered when he walked and he talked very slowly. There was a scar across his face from the slice of vampire fangs.

"They have to feed as soon as they change," he told them. "The vampire who tried to kill me was brand new. There was another one with him, the one who made him into a vampire. He was laughing. My friends staked him. They don't change to dust."

Then he staggered on.

"Wait!" Jilly cried. "Tell us everything you know."

"The new ones are the worst," he said. "They're the most lethal. Just like baby snakes."

Now, as the gloom gathered around them in the rain, they hurried to their old high school. There were lights on and shadows moving in the windows. Neither spoke as they crossed the street and walked past the marquee. The letters had been stolen; there was no school news.

Rose bushes lined the entrance. She couldn't smell their fragrance but the sight of them, drenched by the downpour, gave her a lift. The double doors were painted with crosses; so were the walls and the windows. The taggers had written VAMPIRES SUCK GO TO HELL VAMPIRES on the walls.

There were two guards at the doors—a male teacher named Mr. Vernia and her English teacher, Mary Ann Francis. They hugged both Eli and Jilly hard, asked for news—asked how it was—then ushered them in.

It smelled, and the noise was unbelievable. Students, adults, little kids, and teachers—everyone was milling around; the noise was deafening. People who hated her ran up and hugged her, crying and saying how glad they were that she was alive. She realized she and Eli should have eaten a good meal before they'd come in. If they opened up their pack now, they would have to share.

Is that so bad, sharing?

"Jilly. Eli," their principal, Ms. Howison, said when she spotted them. There were circles under her eyes and deep lines in her forehead. She looked like a skeleton. "Thank God."

Ms. Howison had tried to keep her from coming back to school after rehab. But crises did strange things to people.

Eli skipped the pleasantries and pulled out all his pictures of Sean. Men and women, computer nerds and cheerleaders, carefully examined each one, even if they knew exactly who Sean was, before passing it on. No one had seen him.

Jilly got too tired to stay awake any longer. Principal Howison promised her that all the doors and windows had been covered with crosses and the ground was dotted with garlic bulbs and communion wafers. Jilly wondered if the rain had dissolved the wafers. How many molecules of holiness did you have to have to keep the monsters at bay?

Bazillions of cots were set up in the gym and sure enough, there were Red Cross volunteers. Eli and Jilly pulled two cots together, stashed their packs underneath, and lay down in their clothes. It was better than what she'd been sleeping on before she found Eli, at least.

Eli touched her face with his hands. "I'm so glad you're here."

"Me too," she said, but what she meant was, *I'm so glad you're with me.*

Eli fell asleep. She looked at the diffused light drifting across his face, making him glow. She wanted to kiss him but she didn't want to wake him; correction, she didn't want him to wake up and remind her that he didn't love her that way.

Then she heard someone crying. It was muffled, as if they were trying not to make any noise. She raised her head slightly, and realized it was Ms. Howison.

Jilly disentangled herself from Eli slowly. Then she rocked quietly onto her side, planted her feet underneath herself, and sat up.

She walked over to where the woman was sitting in a chair, facing the rows and rows of cots. She looked as if she'd just thrown up.

"Hey," Jilly said uncertainly, "Ms. Howison."

"Oh, God," she whispered, lowering her gaze to her hands. "Oh, God. Jilly. You're still here. I was hoping. . . ." She turned her head away.

"What?" Jilly asked.

She took a deep breath and let it out. She was shaking like crazy. "I need you to come with me for a second."

"What's wrong?"

"Just . . . come." The principal wouldn't look at her. Jilly shifted. "Please."

Ms. Howison got up out of her chair and walked out of the gym. The overhead fluorescents were on. Jilly followed her past the coaches' offices and then into the girls' locker room, past the rows upon rows of lockers, and then through another door into the shower area.

Ms. Howison cleared her throat and said, "She's here." Then she stepped back and slammed the door between herself and Jilly.

Jilly tried to bolt.

Sean was there, and he was a vampire. All the color in his long, narrow face was gone. His eyes looked glazed, as if he was on drugs. And she should know.

He grabbed her, wrapping his arms around her like a boyfriend; she smelled his breath, like garbage. He wasn't cold; he was room temperature. She was completely numb. Her heart was skipping beats.

She wet her pants.

"I'm glad to see you too," he said, grinning at her.

She set me up. She gave me to him. That bitch.

He wrapped his hand around her bicep and dragged her forward. She burst into tears and started wailing. He clamped his other dead hand still over her mouth so hard she was afraid her front teeth were going to break off.

"Shut up," he hissed, chuckling. "I've wanted to say that to you forever. Shut up, shut up, shut up."

She kept whimpering. She couldn't stop. Maybe he knew that; he dragged her along with his hand over her mouth. His fingernails dug into her arm and she knew he had broken the skin, but she didn't feel it.

He walked her into a storage room where they kept cleaning supplies—brooms, mops, big jugs of cleaner. She started screaming behind his hand, and he slapped her, hard. Then he slammed her against the wall. With a gasp, she bounced back off and fell on her butt.

He slammed the door, leaving her in darkness. With a sob, she crawled to it and started to pound on it.

"*Don't*," he hissed on the other side.

He's going to get Eli, she thought. *Oh, God, he's going to vampirize him. That's what he's here for.*

Maybe he will let me go.

But why would he? He was the King of Bitter. And she would never leave without Eli.

She fumbled around for a light switch, found one, and turned on the blessed, wonderful light. Her arm was bleeding and it finally began to sting. She didn't know if she wanted to feel anything. She wondered what it would be like when he—

The door burst open, and Sean came back inside. His eyes were glittering. He looked crazy. "Eli says hi."

"No," she begged. "Don't do it. Please, Sean. Don't change him."

Sean blinked at her. Then he laughed. "Honey, that's what love is all about, don't you know?"

She doubled up her fists and bit her knuckles. He lifted a brow.

"I smell fresh bloo-ood," he sang. "Yours. It smells *great*. If you were alone in the ocean, the sharks would come and chew you up. Alone in the forest, it would be the wolves. Alone in the city, and it's us."

Vampires. "How . . . how did this happen to you?"

He ignored her. "I'm going to give you a choice, girlfriend. The choice is this: You can change, or he can change. The other one of you . . . is the blood in the water." He moved his shoulders. "I'll let you pick."

She stared at him. "What are you saying?"

"God, you are so stupid. So incredibly, moronically stupid. I could never figure out why he loved you." He shook his head.

Why did it matter, she wondered, when Eli still loved him more?

"Does it even matter which way I choose?" she said. "You don't even like me." Of course he would change Eli and let her die.

"Maybe it doesn't. Maybe I just want to see what you'd say," he told her. "I'm giving him the same choice."

She stared at him in mute terror.

"I told him that I would change you if he asked me to." He folded his arms across his chest and leaned against the back of the door. He didn't look different at all—he was the same surf-charmer Sean.

"You know I'll say to change him," she said. What did she have to live for, after all? Only Eli. And if he were gone. . . .

"Be right back," he said, turning to go.

"Why are you doing this?" she asked.

He didn't turn back around, just looked at her over his shoulder, as if she was being a nuisance.

"I don't know why he's so loyal to you. He doesn't love you the way he loves me."

"But he loves me," she said, as she realized. "That's why. . . ."

He turned around and stared at her. The expression on his face was the most frightening thing she had ever seen. She took another step back, and another. She bumped into the wall.

He raised his chin, opened the door, and left.

She paced. She thought about drinking the cleaner. She tried to break the mops and brooms to make a wooden stake. She couldn't so much as crack one of them.

She fell to her knees and prayed to He/She/It/Them, *Get us out of here get us out of here come in, God, come in, over. . . .*

The door opened, and Sean came back in, grinning like someone who had finally, really, totally gotten what he wanted. Triumph was written all over his face. He looked taller. Meaner.

Ready to kill her.

"Eli will be changing," he said. "GMTA. You both made the same choice."

She jerked. *No, he wouldn't.*

"And you'll be his first meal. Have you ever seen a newly changed vampire? All they want to do is suck someone's blood. That's all I wanted to do."

"You're lying," she said. "Eli would never. . . ."

But Eli *would*. He hadn't even asked her if she wanted to leave his parents' house to help him look for Sean. He had put her in harm's way, for Sean. He didn't love her the way he loved Sean. Lovers did things differently than friends.

"If it makes you feel any better, he feels terrible about it." Sean sneered at her.

"He's going to hate you for making him do this," she said. "He'll never forgive you." She was talking to a vampire. To a vampire who was going to kill her. To a gay vampire who was going to turn Eli into a gay vampire.

She felt reality begin to slip away. This wasn't happening.

"I'm going to get him now," he said, going for a smile, not quite pulling it off. Irritated, he slammed the door.

She stood as still as one of the mops she couldn't turn into a vampire stake. Her heart hammered in her chest and she had no idea how she could hear all that thumping and pumping because she was

at the door

at the door

at the door

pounding and screaming, begging to be let out.

Ms. Howison was going to have a change of heart and rally all the people in the gym and rescue her.

Sean was going to open the door and take her in his arms, and tell her that he'd been so mean to her because he actually loved *her*, not Eli. That he had only pretended to love Eli so he could stay close to her. And that he wouldn't kill either of them, not if Jilly didn't want him to.

Sean was going to tell her that he was sorry, both of them could be changed, and they would go on as they were, as a trio, only nicer, like Dorothy, the Tin Woodsman, and the Scarecrow.

Sean was going to see some other hot guy on the way back to Eli and fall in love with him instead, change him, and leave.

Eli was going to escape, and find her, and they would get out of New York together.

She pounded on the door as she remembered the night Eli had confessed that he had met someone else . . . a guy someone else . . . and he had cried because he didn't want to hurt her, his best friend.

"I will always love you totally and forever, I promise," he had said.

The door opened, and she scrambled backward away from it as fast as she could. Her elbow rammed into a container of cleaner. *Throw it at them. Do something. Save yourself.*

Sean and Eli stood close together. Sean had his arm around Eli, and Eli had on his baggy parka. Eli, as far as she could tell, was still human. His bangs were in his eyes.

He was looking at the floor, as if he couldn't stand to look at her.

"No," she whispered. But it must have been yes, he must have told Sean to change him. Sean was going to change him, and then he was going to kill her.

Her heart broke. She was on the verge of going completely crazy, all over again.

Sean took a step toward her. "If it makes you feel any better, it's going to hurt when I change him," he promised her. He sounded bizarrely sincere.

He shut the door. The three of them stood inside the cramped space. She was only two feet away.

Sean placed both hands on Eli's shoulders and turned Eli toward him. Tears were streaming down Eli's cheeks. He looked young and scared.

Sean threw back his head and hissed. Fangs extended from his mouth.

And Eli whipped his hand into the pocket of his parka; pulling out a jagged strip of wood—

—*Yes!*—

—and he glanced at Jilly—

—*Yes!*—

—and as Sean prepared to sing his fangs into Eli's neck, Jilly rammed Sean as hard as she could. He must have seen it coming, must have guessed—but Eli got the stake into him, dead center in his unbeating heart.

Sean stared down at it, and then at Eli, as blood began to pour down the front of him. Then he laughed, once, and blew Eli a kiss.

He looked at Jilly—gargled, "Bitch," his throat full of his own blood—then slid to the floor like a sack of garbage, inert, harmless.

Eli and Jilly stared at him. Neither spoke. She heard Eli panting.

Then Eli gathered her up. Kissed her.

Kissed her.

They clung to each other beside the dead vampire. And Eli threw himself over Sean, holding *him*, kissing *him*.

"Oh, my God, Sean," he keened. "Oh, God, oh, God. *Jilly.*" He reached for her hand. She gave it to him, wrapping herself around him as he started to wail.

After he wore himself out, she tried to get up, thinking to see if there were more vampires, to check on Ms. Howison and the others, but he held her too tightly, and she wouldn't have moved away from him for the world.

He held Sean tightly too. "I can't believe it. How evil he was." Eli's voice was hoarse from all the sobbing.

"I know," she said. "He was always—"

"Sean wasn't even in there. When you're changed, the vampirism infects you and steals your soul," Eli went on. "You're not there. You're gone."

Tears clung to the tip of his nose.

"Sean loved you, Jilly. He told me that a million times every day. He was so glad you're my best friend."

She started to say, "No, he hated me," but suddenly she realized: that was going to be his coping mechanism. He was going to believe from now on that the Sean he knew and loved would have never made him kill his best friend.

She put her hand on the crown of his head and found herself thinking of the tapestry of the Jews at Masada in his parents' living room. It was a pivotal moment in Jewish history, when cornered Jewish soldiers chose to leap over a cliff rather than submit to Roman rule. Mr. Stein talked about it now and then, and sometimes Jilly had wondered if what he was saying was that Eli should take his own life, rather than be gay. She couldn't believe that, though, couldn't stand even to suspect it. The rigidity of the adult world was what had made her crazy. The unbelievable insanity of Mr. Stein, who condemned his own son just because Eli couldn't change into a heterosexual Jewish warrior and defy the invading sin of misplaced lust. At least, that was what her therapist had told her.

"You are brilliant, and you're so . . . *much*," Dr. Robles had declared. Dr. Robles, her savior. "People don't change, Jilly. They just see things differently than they used to, and respond according to the way they already are. It's all context. Reality. Is. Context."

Dr. Robles had saved her because he didn't try to change her. So she had never tried to change Eli.

She took a deep breath and thought about her hopeless love for him. And something shifted.

Her love was *not* hopeless. She loved him. It didn't have to break her heart. It didn't have to do anything but be there. Be there.

So she said, "Sean loved you so much." Because that would help him the most.

"Thank you," he whispered. "He loved you too. And I love you, Jilly." He looked up at her, broken and crumpled like a rag—the boy she kissed in the eighth grade, a thousand million times, almost until her lips bled.

"And I love you," she replied. "I love you more than my own life. I always have." It was right to say that now. People didn't change, and love didn't, either. Where Eli was concerned, there was no context.

"Thank you," he said. No embarrassment, no apologies; their love was what it was. Alone in a closet, with a dead vampire, hiding in a school because the rest of the city was overrun by vampires. . . .

She laid her head on his shoulder, and he laced his fingers with hers.

"Happy birthday, sweet sixteen," he whispered. "My Jilly girl."

"Thank you," she whispered. It was the best present ever.

After a while, they opened the door. The sun was out, and for one instant, she thought she heard the trilling of a lark.

Then she realized that it was Eli's cell phone.

Beepbeepbeepbeep. This is God, Jilly. I'm back on the job amen.

Blue Moon

RICHELLE MEAD

I was trapped.

I'd thought this back door led to freedom. Instead, I found myself in a narrow alley, the only other exit leading back to the main road where cops and others were looking for me. What was I going to do? I hesitated, wondering if the street was safer than going back through the club. Before I could decide, though, I heard a a door close behind me. I spun around.

There was a human standing there. A guy. He looked like he was about my age, maybe a little older. His brown hair was a bit shaggy for my tastes, but his eyes were beautiful. They were a deep, deep green. Like the color emeralds are supposed to be but never are. When I looked at him, the weirdest jolt went through me. He was cute, but it wasn't physical attraction that suddenly gave me pause. It was more like a sense of recognition, as though I'd known him for years. That made no sense; I'd never seen him before. I shook off the feeling, and, as my eyes swept his body, I saw something else even more beautiful: a purple badge clipped to his belt.

"Get me out of here," I said, mustering as much harshness as I could, given the circumstances. If he worked at this club—and his clothing suggested he did—then he was used to taking orders from vampires. "Take me to your car."

I waited for him to cower, for his eyes to go wide. Maybe he'd gulp or give me a shaky nod. Instead, he frowned and asked, "Why?"

I stared, momentarily at a loss for words. "Because I told you to!"

Those beautiful eyes assessed me the way mine had just done him. "You're afraid," he said, more puzzled than anything else. "Why? Vampires are never afraid."

"I'm *not* afraid—but I'm going to get mad if you don't do what I tell you to do." Desperate, I reached into my purse and pulled out a wad of cash. I didn't bother to count it, but there were some hundreds on top. "Will you stop asking questions if I give you this?"

This time, his eyes did go wide. He hesitated only a moment and then snatched the money from my hand. "Come on."

I followed him back inside the club. I'd entered earlier through its main door, cutting through mobs of people writhing to heavy techno beats. This guy took me down another hall, one that led past a kitchen and some storage rooms. At the hallway's end was another outside door. He pushed it open, revealing a darkened parking lot surrounded by a wire fence.

He unlocked a rusty Honda Civic, and I scurried in, nervously glancing around me. Aside from the silent cars, the parking lot was empty. For the first time tonight, I allowed myself the brief hope that I might actually get out of this alive.

"What's your name?" I asked.

"Nathan," he said, glancing behind him as he backed out of the parking spot. "You?"

"Lucy." A moment later, I silently cursed myself for giving my real name. What was I thinking? I gave him a sidelong glance, wondering if the name meant anything to him—it had been all over the news, after all—but he appeared to be too preoccupied with driving.

We pulled out onto the main road, and I slouched in my seat. This was a party district. Groups of people were everywhere. Some walked along the street, going from club to club. Some were already in line at the clubs—humans, of course. Vampires rarely had to wait to get in.

I scanned the crowds, looking for any sign of my pursuers and finding none. Not that that meant anything. Bryan had a vast network of agents working for him, men and women who moved with stealth and speed unusual even among vampires.

"Okay, Lucy," said Nathan, still not sounding very respectful. "Where do you want me to drop you off at?"

"Lakemont."

"Lake—what? That's almost two hours away!"

"For the amount of money I gave you, you should drive me somewhere twelve hours away."

"I have to get back to work! I'm on break. I thought I was just dropping you off somewhere."

"You are. Lakemont."

"No way. I can't be gone for four hours. I'll lose my job."

"Get another one."

He scoffed. "Oh, great. That's so typical of you vamps. 'Get another one.' Like it's that easy."

"That money I gave you is more than you make in a week," I snapped. "Probably even a month."

"Yeah, but what about after that?"

"Look," I said. "You don't have a choice here. Either take me to Lakemont, or go ahead and *try* to drop me off somewhere. As soon as you stop the car, I'm going to rip your throat out."

It was an empty threat. I didn't need to feed, nor did I have any intention to when there were so many other things to worry about right now. Still, I hoped I sounded scary and convincing.

Nathan didn't answer. He also didn't stop the car. After several minutes of quiet driving, he said, "We'll never get through the checkpoints."

"You have a purple badge." It was the reason I'd forced him to help me, after all. "You must commute in and out of the city."

"I do. *I* can get through. You could too—technically. But something tells me you don't actually want the patrols to see you."

My stomach sank. I hadn't thought of that. "Maybe I can hide in the trunk."

He laughed, though there was a hint of bitterness in it. Weirdly, something about the sound of his laughter still sent a pleasant tingle down my spine. Too bad I was the one he was laughing at. "You've never had to be stopped and searched at the checkpoints, have you?"

"They'll search the trunk?"

"Sometimes. They do random checks a lot. And if they think there's something suspicious going on, then they'll definitely check."

I turned away and leaned my cheek against the window. The glass was cool against my skin. Hot tears welled up in my eyes, and I blinked rapidly to send them away. No way was I going to cry in front of him.

"Why are you running away?"

"It doesn't matter," I said. Bad enough vampires knew. I couldn't risk letting a human find out.

"Okay, whatever."

"You don't even care. You're just doing this for the money anyway."

"I'm doing it because you threatened to rip my throat out."

"*And* for the money."

He gave a half-shrug, his eyes fixed on the road ahead. "If you're in big enough trouble, maybe I'd get more for turning you in."

I actually had a feeling he would, so I again tried my best to sound fierce. I'd never actually had to force humans to do things for me before. They'd always just kind of . . . done them. "These people after me are vampires. Not humans. If you think I'm dangerous, wait'll you see them. And if they think you helped me escape—and they will—getting paid is going to be the last thing on your mind."

More silence fell between us, and I realized we were already on the freeway. Maybe I was better at this than I thought.

"You got more money?" he asked.

"Why? Are you raising your rates?"

"Answer the question if you actually want to leave the city."

"Yeah. I have more."

"A lot more?"

"Yes. A lot more. How much do you need?"

His answer was to get off at the next exit and start heading back in the direction we'd come from.

"What are you doing?" I exclaimed.

"Getting you out of the city."

He took us to a part of town I'd rarely been in. Mostly humans lived there, but naturally, vampires ran it. It was dirty and rundown and not a place I'd feel safe walking around if I were a human.

Nathan pulled the car up in front of a shop with a window that said TATTOOS in neon letters.

"Okay. Let's see the rest of your money."

I dug into my purse and handed over my cash. He raised an eyebrow.

"Wow. You weren't kidding." He counted out half of it and then, to my surprise, gave me back the rest. "Hang on to this."

Puzzled but intrigued, I followed him into the tattoo parlor. Loud rock music blared at us. Through an open doorway, I caught a glimpse of a bald man wielding what I assumed were tattooist's needles in a backroom. At the counter, a man with a Mohawk laughed with a heavily pierced girl over some joke. They glanced up at us.

"Nate, you bastard," said the man, still laughing. "Long time no—" His smile faded as he took a good look at me and saw my eyes. The girl visibly paled. Both of them straightened up. The man grabbed a remote control and hastily shut off the loud music, so that the only sound came from a small TV sitting behind them. "Hello, miss. Is there something we can help you with?"

Nathan laughed and—to my complete and utter surprise— threw an arm around me. The smell of his skin and sweat washed over me—and it was delicious. "Relax with the yes-sir-no-sir stuff, Pete. She's with me—doing a little human slumming this weekend."

Some of the tension went out of them, but they were still eyeing me nervously. "Well, good for you, Nate," said Pete, not entirely sounding like he meant it.

"Think you can make her human?" Nathan asked.

Pete smiled and nudged the girl. "Oh, into that, huh? Sure, Donna can do that. Contacts and everything?"

"The works." Nathan's entire posture was relaxed, his smile easy and natural. He was a completely different person than the one who'd been in the car. Of course, I'd threatened to rip his throat out in the car, so the difference was understandable. Meanwhile, I was trying not to think about how good he smelled. "Something else . . ." Nathan touched the badge on his belt. "I don't suppose you could make a purple?"

Pete's tension returned. "Whoa, that's a bit out of the norm."

"We can pay."

Pete glanced between the two of us. "It's for *her*? Why does she need it? How far are you taking the role-playing?"

"Nothing like that. I just want to take her home with me—but we can't let anyone know. She's got a jealous boyfriend."

"Sounds like a lot of trouble and money. Easier to just stay in the city."

"Can you do it or not?"

"Yeah . . . take me about an hour or so, and you know it's never as exact as the real thing. You get caught—"

"—and I won't say where I got it," finished Nathan. "I know the drill."

Pete went to the backroom to make our counterfeit badge and told Donna to give me the works. She beckoned me over but I turned back toward Nathan and gripped his shirt, pulling him slightly toward me.

"What's going on?" I hissed. "You guys make it sound like a common thing, vampires dressing up like humans."

"Wow, you really are an innocent, aren't you?" He seemed genuinely amused. "Don't you know any vamps who do it?"

I frowned. "No. Why would they? Like . . . for costume parties?"

"No. Because it's a turn-on for them."

"Ew."

"People are into weird things." He pointed toward Donna. "Go."

Donna was a little older than me—maybe in her twenties—and had obviously bleached-blond hair and too much eye shadow. As she worked, it was clear she was afraid of me. Conversation eventually dropped, except for when Nathan made the occasional remark on our progress.

"What color do you want?" she asked at one point.

"Color what?"

"Contacts. Your eyes."

I didn't know what to say. It was something I'd never even thought about, changing my eye color. My eyes were silver, just like every other vampire's. For a moment, I considered Nathan's beautiful green, but that didn't seem right. Those were *his* eyes.

"How about blue?" said Donna impatiently. "You seem like you could do blue."

"Blue," I repeated weakly.

She retrieved a pack of contacts and spent the next half-hour trying to help me get them into my eyes. I couldn't use a mirror, and I liked neither my own fingers nor hers poking me. Once the contacts were in, she applied a bit more makeup and finished just as Pete returned. He took my picture with a digital camera and then disappeared with Donna into the back to finish the badge.

Nathan walked over and checked me out. "Not bad. You make a cute human. Just don't smile and show your fangs."

"I don't look like Donna, do I? Her makeup's horrible." I realized how that sounded. "Oh, sorry. She's not a friend of yours, is she?"

"Your makeup's fine. And no, I've never met her. Pete's always got a different girlfriend."

"Is he your friend?"

"Kind of. We used to work together at a restaurant when I was in high school. Then he got some money and opened up this place."

"Are you in college now?"

"I should be." I immediately regretted asking him because that easy humor he'd shown since we'd come in disappeared. Bitterness replaced it. "No money. Besides, I spent so much time working in high school that my grades sucked. I'm not good enough to get an academic scholarship and not connected enough to get a vamp endorsement."

I was about to say that I could talk to my father, that he could probably get Nathan an endorsement. It was something vampires did if they wanted favored humans to be trained or educated for a certain position. These humans breezed through the college admissions process and had all their expenses paid for.

I swallowed off the comment, suddenly remembering everything that had happened. I could hardly talk to my father about that. In fact, it was unlikely I'd ever talk to him again. Instead, I told Nathan, "I'm sorry."

"Unbelievable. I've never heard a vampire apologize in my life. And now I've heard you do it twice since we've been—"

The words dropped off as his eyes focused on something behind me. Confused, I turned around . . .

. . . and looked into my own face on the TV.

Seeing my image was always a little surreal. Since vampires cast no reflections, we'd had no way of seeing our own appearances for eons. With the advent of technology like video and photographs, we'd finally gotten a way to see what we looked like.

They'd picked a horrible photo of me. I had dark circles under my eyes that made my skin look whiter than usual. Even on film, the clear silvery-gray of my vampiric eyes showed through. My hair— plain, boring brown—looked like it hadn't been brushed that day. Where *had* they found that picture?

"Ugh," I said. Underneath the image, a perky blond reporter delivered news of my disappearance.

"Today, authorities are looking for Lucy Wade, daughter of Chicago philanthropist and business owner Douglas Wade. Lucy disappeared earlier this evening after a fight with her parents. She is described as a troubled teen, one with a history of drug abuse and stints of running away."

"What?" I exclaimed. "I've never touched drugs in my life!"

"She was last seen on St. Jane Avenue, entering Club Fathom. If anyone has information to offer about Ms. Wade, they should contact the police. Her family says they're anxious to get Lucy the help she needs and are offering a reward for any assistance."

Nathan turned on me. "What the hell? You're Lucy *Wade*?" He spoke low enough so the others wouldn't hear, but the anger came through loud and clear.

There was no avoiding it. "Yeah, I guess I am."

He threw up his hands and began pacing the room. "Oh my God. Oh my *God*. I helped hide Douglas Wade's fugitive daughter. Douglas Wade! He owns Fathom. He's like, my boss's boss's boss."

"I know."

"He owns this town!"

"I know!"

"You made it sound like you were some wronged victim, and really, your parents just want to put you back in rehab!"

"No," I said. "That's not true. All of that stuff she just said is a lie."

Nathan spun around, face still angry. "I knew I shouldn't have trusted a vamp. What are you, part of some conspiracy, and they're trying to keep you quiet?"

"You'd be surprised."

"Tell me then."

"I . . . can't. I can't tell anyone. I know something I'm not supposed to, and they want to kill me for it. They *will* kill me, Nathan. My own family."

It was like I hadn't spoken. "Jesus Christ. I'm helping the junkie daughter of one of the most powerful vamps in town. I should just walk away now. If you do kill me, it's no worse than what they're going to do when they find me."

I jumped off my chair and ran up to him. "No. Please. Don't. Look, you don't even have to take me to Lakemont. Just drop me off as soon as we cross the border."

He looked down at me, his eyes like green flames. There was so much rage there, so much frustration. I had the uneasy feeling that when he looked at me, he was seeing years of vampire abuse. A lifetime's worth, really. My kind had come out of hiding and started their occupation of the human world before he was born. Before today, I'd never really thought what it must be like to live under another race's rule—a race that you had almost no hope of defeating. We were stronger, faster, and could only be killed by a stake through the heart—which humans could almost never get close enough for. I had no clue what Nathan had been through.

"Please," I whispered. "You can have all the rest of the money."

He stared at me for several more heavy moments, and as he did, something shifted in that angry expression. I couldn't explain it, but I suddenly knew he'd had that same weird feeling I'd had in the alley. Like there was a connection between us, some longtime familiarity. He sighed. Turning away, he flipped off the TV. "Last thing I need is for Pete to see that. Hopefully, I can get rid of you before anyone realizes I was anywhere near you. He should be just about done."

But after ten miserable minutes of silence passed, Nathan finally eyed the doorway with suspicion. He walked over to it and stuck his head in. "Pete?" No answer came, and Nathan ventured farther in. Thirty seconds later, he came tearing out of the room. He grabbed my arm and jerked me toward the main door. I was so surprised that I stumbled along with him. If I'd wanted to, my strength would have stopped him from even budging me.

"What's going on?" I asked as we stepped back outside.

"They're all gone. There was a TV on back there too. My guess is they saw the story, sold us out, and then took off."

We slid into the car, and he started up the engine. Once we'd pulled away from the curb and were on the road, he handed me the fake badge. They'd apparently finished it and then abandoned it. It said my name was Sara Brown, that I was an eighteen-year-old human, and that I had work clearance to cross out of the city to the suburbs. Most intriguing of all was the picture. Donna had done a good job of diminishing some of my paleness. I wasn't fake-baked or anything, but there was definitely a human-like color to my face. And the eyes . . . the eyes were exquisite. They were a clear, pale blue. I was entranced.

"At least we didn't have to pay for it," I pointed out.

"Not that it does us a lot of good. We can't cross over."

"Why not?"

"Pete would have told the police I was with you. By now, they've pulled up everything there is to know about me—including my car and license plate. Every checkpoint knows we're coming and what we'll be in."

The urge to cry returned, and I again shoved it back. I tried hard to be strong and think of a solution on my own.

"Can we steal a car?"

He cut me a look. "Do you know how to?"

"Well, no."

"Do you think I know how to? You think that's something all lower class humans know how to do? That we're all criminals?"

"Well, no . . . of course not. I mean—"

"But," he interrupted, "you might be on to something." He abruptly pulled over to the curb and opened the car door. "Come on."

I scurried out after him. "What are we doing?"

"Finding other transportation."

We cut through a parking lot and ended up on a street that reminded me of the one Club Fathom was on. Only, much like in the tattoo parlor's neighborhood, everything here was dirtier and plainer. We stood off to the side, and Nathan studied the crowds. People who walked past us didn't give us a second glance. We were both just ordinary humans.

Finally, his eyes landed on two guys walking out of a bar. One held a set of keys and a bit of purple showed near his waist. Nathan took my hand, and we ran up to them. He turned the smile back on.

"Hey, man, are you guys going out of the city?" Nathan flashed them his purple badge.

One of the guys was clearly drunk, and the other (the driver, I hoped) looked like he was in a good mood. "Yeah, out to Evanston."

"Our car broke down," said Nathan. "And there's no way we can get it fixed before curfew. Can we bum a ride with you? Doesn't matter where you drop us off—just get us out, and then I'll call my friends."

The two guys exchanged glances, then looked back at us. "Sure," said the sober one. "No problem." They must have decided we were harmless enough. Little did they know.

Once we were on the road, the two guys talked to each other, practically forgetting we were in the backseat.

"What did you want to study in college?" I asked Nathan, keeping my voice low. "Drama?"

He'd been staring out the window, face stormy, no doubt pondering how I'd ruined his life. "Huh?"

"You're doing a pretty good acting job with everyone," I explained.

He gave me a bitter smile. "When you could potentially be killed by a vamp mob boss, you suddenly get really good at acting. But for the record? You're terrible. I never actually believed you were going to rip my throat out."

"Oh," I said, hearing the disappointment in my own voice.

"You aren't eighteen yet, are you?"

"No."

"How much longer until you are?"

"Less than a year."

A bit of worry crossed his features. "Oh. You could still make a kill now."

"I won't. I'm . . . I'm going to wait."

All vampires had to have their first feeding by the time they turned eighteen, and there were times I felt that desire for blood waking up, even though the thought of actually killing someone in cold blood terrified me. That was why I was in no rush for the kill—that and I had a few other things on my mind, like staying alive. My mom wouldn't get to throw her big first-kill party for me. Of course, if Bryan and the others caught me soon, maybe my parents could just use the decorations and caterers for my funeral.

I moved the subject back. "So, what would you study in college?"

"Mmm. I don't know. Something different. Something with meaning. Something that could change the world." There was an inspired, almost wistful look on his face. A moment later, he seemed to replay his words and grow embarrassed at having admitted something so idealist and vulnerable. His face darkened. "Something that isn't a bartender."

"Well, even if you can't go to college . . . maybe you could do some other kind of work?"

He shook his head, expression darkening once more. "There you go again, Lucy. You still don't see what it's like, not from your position."

"Why is it so hard? You're smart and nice and obviously resourceful. Why can't you do something else?"

He seemed a little surprised at the compliments, but that didn't sidetrack him. "You're a vampire. You're at the top of the food chain. Our master. *You* can do anything you want. You can kill us if you want, and really, there are no consequences."

"The lottery—"

"Oh, come on. Even you can't be naïve enough to believe that the lottery is *always* followed."

To ration our food supply, we'd instituted an annual feeding system. Certain populations of humans—criminals, the poor, other undesirables—were put into a pool and when each vampire's feeding time came, he or she drew a name. It was why the border between the city and the suburbs was so strictly regulated. It made it easier to track down the "winners." Who got put into the pool was sketchy sometimes, and as he had pointed out, the system wasn't always followed. Plenty of vampires indulged in non-regulatory snacks, even if it was technically illegal. But when humans disappeared, few people asked questions.

"I can see why you hate us," I said feebly.

He turned back to the window. "No. You really can't."

"Do you hate me?"

"I don't know what I think of you. You've probably destroyed my life. I should turn you in at the border . . . and yet . . ."

"What?"

He sighed. "I don't know. There's something weird about you. Something . . . well, I can't explain it. It's like I've known you for a long time. God, that sounds so stupid."

Not entirely stupid. I knew exactly what he meant, though I still didn't understand it either.

For the rest of the drive, I just sat back and thought. My whole life had changed. Everything I'd expected to do with it seemed impossible now. In my mind's eye, I could still see the disc, that beautiful circle embossed with gold and silver, covered in swirls and shapes that everyone assumed were nonsensical designs created by a long-dead vampire artisan. But when I'd looked at it, the symbols had spoken to me. Looking at them was like reading a billboard. The message had come through to me loud and clear—and everyone had realized it. My father and Bryan had acted quickly, and I'd barely managed to escape.

"Here we are," said Nathan, interrupting my thoughts.

The car slowed down, and ahead, I recognized the signs of a border checkpoint. Long stretches of cruel, barbed fences. Towering, blinding lamp posts. My heart raced as I recalled what Nathan had said about random checks.

He and I handed our badges to the driver. A moment later, a vampire in a uniform peered through the open window,. He looked bored, probably at the end of his shift and tired of inspecting cars. He skimmed through the stack of badges, hardly even looking at them. Hope surged in me. Pete would have tipped the authorities off to my fake badge name, but border security was probably paying a lot more attention to cars with just a guy and a girl. The vampire handed the badges back and then shone a flashlight on all of our faces. It lingered on mine, and suddenly, he looked a little less bored. After a few moments of studying me, the guard said, "Pull through to the holding area." He stepped back, pointing to a spot off to the side of the wooden gate that admitted traffic.

"Damn it," said the guy driving. He didn't sound scared so much as annoyed. "I just want to get home."

I shot Nathan a panicked look. He placed a reassuring hand on mine, seemed surprised, and took it back. "This happens. It's random."

We got out of the car, and a bored-looking uniformed woman searched it. Meanwhile, the guy who'd looked in the window searched us. He had everyone turn out their pockets, and then he felt each of us down. I was the last one he came to. I tensed, fearing recognition, and then suddenly realized that wasn't what I needed to be afraid of.

He pushed me up against the passenger side of the car, standing so close that there was almost no space between us. I felt trapped, suffocated. Then, when his hands began running up and down my body, I thought I would scream. He spent much longer 'searching' me than he had the others, far more interested in my body itself than anything I might be hiding on it. Beyond him, I saw Nathan glowering.

"Will you hurry up?" asked the other guard, clearly annoyed.

"Hang on," said my guard. "She seems dangerous."

I knew I was trembling and hated myself for it, even though it was what a human would probably do. A human girl would stand there, afraid, and take this humiliation. That was all I had to do. It'd be over soon if I could just be patient.

But when his hands slid under my shirt and up to the bottom edge of my bra, I snapped. Anger burst up inside of me. Before he realized what was happening, I lashed out and grabbed him, throwing him as far and as hard as I could into the small brick building that stood at the border. We both had the same vampiric strength and reflexes, but I'd caught him totally unprepared. He hit the wall with a *thwack* and slumped to the ground, unmoving. His face was dazed and blank, but I knew I hadn't killed him. He would heal soon, just like all vampires did.

The woman stood there, stunned for a moment. Then her eyes widened with recognition. "Lucy Wade," she exclaimed, just before leaping out at me.

I blocked her attack as best I could. We were close in size, but she'd been trained to fight, and I hadn't. I hit the side of the car with a jolt, rattling my teeth. She came at me again while yelling for backup. I swung at her with a very bad punch. I missed her face but hit her shoulder, which made her stagger a little. Any minute now, reinforcements would show up or the guy I'd thrown was going to get up.

Suddenly, I heard a car door slam. From the driver's side window, I heard Nathan yell, "Lucy, get in!" The engine started up.

I dodged a punch. Eyeing the woman carefully, I waited for her next swing. It came, and I dropped to the ground and scrambled away. I made it to the other side of the car, but she was only footsteps behind. I slid into the backseat on the driver's side. She reached for me, and I slammed the door on her hand. She screamed in pain and jerked back. I shut the door.

She beat on the side of the car, but Nathan hit the gas, heading straight toward the wooden gate. We hit it. The impact pushed my head sharply against the backseat, but we kept on going through a shower of splinters. I suspected the car's front didn't look so good.

I righted myself from my sprawl. "You're insane," I said. Peering around him, I saw that we were going about eighty. I glanced back, half-expecting to see flashing lights. There were none yet, but it could only be a matter of time.

"Me? You're the one who decided to take on the border patrol."

"That guy was a pervert."

"They're all like that," said Nathan. "Well, okay. They're not all the girl-molesting types, but that kind of stuff goes on all the time—and things a lot worse than that too."

"Thanks for another lesson on how terrible vampires are."

I couldn't see his face, but I had a feeling he looked sheepish. "Are . . . are you okay?"

"Yeah. He didn't do much." Something warm swirled in me at the thought that Nathan might actually be worried about me.

The car suddenly swerved off onto an angling road, and I slid to the side, just barely putting my hands out in time to brace myself.

"What are you doing?" I asked.

"You still want to go to Lakemont?"

Did I? *We can help you. We'll protect you.* The words echoed in my mind.

"Yeah."

"Then we can't take the main road. There's going to be an army coming after us."

Even off the freeway, Nathan kept up an aggressive speed. We rode in silence for a long time, and finally, I asked, "What happened?"

"Hmm?"

"Something happened to you. It's why you hate vampires."

"What, you haven't seen enough tonight to figure out why I'd hate you guys?"

Yes, I certainly had. And it was bothering me. I'd played human for less than two hours and learned more than I wanted to about the interactions between our races. And yet, that strange sense I had about Nathan told me there was something more that I needed to hear.

"But I want to know what happened to *you*."

I thought for sure he'd ignore me. Finally, he talked.

"When I was about twelve, there were these vampires who kept giving my brother Adam a hard time. He was, oh, ten, I think. They lived a few streets over—in a much nicer neighborhood—but used to come over to ours to cause trouble. They kept beating him up—never killed him or tried to feed off him. My other brother and I tried to stop them. We were pretty good fighters, but that doesn't matter when you're going up against that kind of strength. They'd just brush us aside. They weren't really interested in us. I think they just liked going after Adam because he was so small. They thought it was funny. Finally, my dad went and complained to their parents."

"And?"

"And, just like that, my dad was blacklisted. He got fired from his job, and no one else would hire him. My mom had to work, but she didn't have it much easier than my dad did. What she was finally able to get hardly earned anything, and so as the rest of us got older, we all started working too." The expression on his face made me think he wasn't even seeing me anymore. He was off in his memories, reliving events from years ago. "The thing is, not long after my dad complained, those guys came back for my brother—and they had a lot more of their friends. They cornered him alone one night and just pummeled him."

"Did they—did he—"

"Die? No. But he was in really bad shape. He had to go to the hospital. Another bill we couldn't afford. They broke his leg—shattered the bone in some weird way. The doctor technically reset it, but . . . well, it never healed right, and he has a permanent limp."

"'Technically reset it?'"

"Well, yeah. We're pretty sure the doctor, even though he was human, was on a vamp's payroll and told not to treat it properly." He paused. Preparing himself for the next part? "Not long after that, my uncle was taken."

"Taken?"

"For the lottery. He didn't meet the criteria, but . . . well, he ended up in the pool anyway. And one day, he was just gone."

I leaned my head back. "That's horrible. You were right."

"Right about what?"

"Earlier . . . I said I could understand why you hated us, and you said I couldn't. You were right. There's no way I could—no way I probably ever could. You mean it—*really* mean it—when you say you hate vampires. I get that now."

"Yes, Lucy. I hate them. I really hate them. If I had the power to kill every vampire in the world and make things the way they used to be, I would." There was venom in his voice, and even though there was no way he could kill me, I felt afraid.

"I would too," I said.

"Would what?"

"Hate vampires."

Long silence followed. "I never expected to hear a vampire say that."

"Nathan . . . why are you helping me?"

"I don't know," he said, sounding as confused as me. "Maybe it's because other vampires hate you, and by helping you, I'm getting back at them. Maybe it's because I'm trapped in this and have no choice. Maybe it's because I keep saying horrible things about you and your kind, but you're still nice to me. Maybe it's because. . . ."

My breath caught. In the midst of all this chaos tonight, some tiny part of me hoped he'd say something as sweet and simple as, *Because I like you.* "Because?"

"I don't know. I can't explain it, and it's driving me crazy."

The rest of the drive passed uneventfully. No pursuers. Thanks to Nathan's side route, it almost seemed like we might pull this off.

Lakemont arrived much more quickly than expected. I gave Nathan the address I had, and we drove around for a while looking for it. It turned out to be a small house set at the far end of a fancy subdivision overlooking Lake Michigan. The neighborhood was still under construction, so some houses were half-finished and some were simply empty lots. We pulled into the driveway and stared at the house for several moments.

"Now what?" Nathan asked.

"Now we go in. Or, well, I do. You don't have to come with me."

"Is it safe?"

I thought back to the terrified vampire who'd found me just as things were blowing up back home. He'd whispered that he knew what was going on and that there were others who wanted to help me and keep me safe. He'd given me this address and then disappeared, frightened of discovery. I didn't blame him.

"These people are going to help me," I said. "They know what's going on."

"I'm glad somebody does."

"I'm sorry," I said, meaning it. I got out of the car, and several moments later, Nathan followed. He didn't look very happy.

We rang the bell and waited. An old human woman, a servant presumably, looked out at us in confusion.

"I'm Lucy," I said.

She studied me longer, then laughed shakily. "I didn't recognize you, Miss Wade. The eyes are very clever. Come in. You and your . . . friend. You're safe now."

We stepped inside a very ordinary-looking house. There was no furniture in it yet; it must have just been constructed. There were no lights on either, but vampires wouldn't need them. We followed our guide into the living room, our footsteps echoing on the wood floors.

Ten other people were in the living room, all in suits, and even with my eyes, I couldn't make out their faces very well. Uneasiness started to crawl down my spine. I'd focused so hard on getting here, convincing myself I'd be safe . . . now I wondered if I was as naïve as Nathan kept saying. These vampires could be here to kill me—though it seemed terribly elaborate. The guy who'd given me the address could have just killed me back in Chicago.

"We aren't going to hurt you," said a short woman. "We want to keep you safe, Lucy. My name's Laurel."

"What are you going to do?" I asked.

"Get you out of here. When daylight comes, we'll bundle you up and smuggle you out in a van so that no one can find you."

"Why are you doing this for her?" asked Nathan. "Why do you care?"

"Because we know Lucy's being pursued unfairly," said Laurel. "And you are . . . ?"

"None of your business. And she's not going anywhere with you until we know what's going on." His manner was protective and fierce.

I wanted to tell him there was no need for bravery, except I honestly wasn't sure. Laurel laughed and shifted slightly. A patch of light from outside fell over her face. Her eyes still looked dark. *Dark.* Not silver.

Realizing what I'd discovered, Laurel moved at the same time I did. I locked into a defensive posture, expecting attack, but it was Nathan she grabbed. She put a gun to his head and jerked him toward her. The men with her all pulled out guns of their own and encircled her. I looked from shadowy face to shadowy face, trying to figure out how to get us out of here. This was a strange twist. My father and Bryan had sent humans after me.

"Nathan's not involved with this," I said. "He doesn't know anything."

"Cooperate, and we'll let him go," Laurel said. "You have no real choice."

"I'm not letting you take me back to my parents!"

"Your parents? My dear, we have no intention of taking you back to your people so that they can kill you. We want you alive—we want you very alive."

I understood then. How could I have been so stupid? So naïve? When I'd originally believed these were vampires who wanted to help me, I'd assumed it was because they didn't believe in the prophecy and pitied me. Upon discovering they were humans, I'd believed they'd been sent by my father. Plenty of vampires had humans working for them. The whole time, I'd been blind to one simple fact: The reason all these vampires wanted me to die was the very same reason humans would want me to live. "Yes," she said, no doubt seeing the understanding on my face. "We know. We know about the disc and the blue moon. Come with us, and we'll make sure you stay alive. We want to help you."

"You want to use me." They were some kind of human anti-vampire resistance group, people who were trying to "change the world" and eradicate vampires—just like Nathan wanted to do.

"The way I understand it, you benefit too. Wouldn't that be nice? Being able to go in the sun? Not needing blood?"

"I'm not going to kill my own people!"

"They're trying to kill you," said one of the men.

He was right, and it was something I'd been thinking about all day. I'd said—*swore*—I'd never fulfill the prophecy. But the more this went on, the more I started to wonder. Why was I trying to save people who wanted me dead? And yet, as angry as that made me, I knew falling in with Laurel's group wasn't the right course of action. They didn't care what I wanted either. I was only a weapon to them.

"What are you talking about?" said Nathan. "Why would she kill her own people?"

Laurel pressed the barrel closer to his head. "Tell him, Lucy. Tell him the story."

"Let him go," I repeated.

"I told you I would if you cooperated. I want to hear this from your lips. I want you to tell us everything you know."

"Lucy . . ."

Nathan's eyes were wide with fear and confusion. He was worried about me, I realized, worried about me even with a gun against his own head.

"You don't have to tell them anything, Lucy," he said.

But I had to. His life was on the line—and it was all my fault. I swallowed. "I can kill them. All of them."

"All of who?"

"The vampires."

"Vampires can already kill vampires."

"I can make it so humans can kill vampires." Saying it out loud hurt. It made it more real, and I'd been trying so hard tonight to keep it out of my mind, to deny what I was. What I could do. "There's this prophecy we've always had. No one really believed it. It said one vampire would be born during the blue moon—you know, when a month is long and has an extra full moon in it? That vampire's eighteenth birthday will also occur during a blue moon. That's me. Both birthdays falling on a blue moon."

Nathan was riveted. The other humans were too, no doubt having longed to hear this for some time.

"That could apply to a lot of people," Nathan said hesitantly.

"There's more. We have this thing in a museum—it's thousands of years old. A disc with a bunch of writing on it—but no one can read it. It's gibberish. Except I can. I looked at it, and it made perfect sense. It told me how humans can destroy vampires."

"No one's been able to do that. . . ." I could hear the wonder in his voice, and I remembered his words from earlier, talking about how he'd do anything to kill vampires. "But why would anyone think you'd help do it?"

"The prophecy says I have the power to transform humans into vampire killers—people who'd have the same strength and powers as us, maybe more. And that after I create thirteen . . . something will happen to me. I'll still have all my strength and long life but none of the side effects. I'll be able to go out in the daylight. I won't need blood."

"So they think you'd sell them out because of that. They're afraid and want to get you out of the picture, so you don't ruin their rule. And *this* group wants you so that you can bring humans back into power."

"You're one of us, Nathan," said Laurel. "You should see the opportunity here."

"She doesn't want to conquer either race," he retorted. "You should leave her alone."

I'd been sizing the group up the whole time we spoke, looking for any weakness I could use. I'd come up with a few options when the windows behind them suddenly shattered.

And vampires swooped in.

I couldn't believe I'd ever mistaken these humans for vampires. My people were fast and graceful, instantly spreading out. There were as many of them as the humans, but I knew who would win this fight.

"Hello, Lucy," said a familiar voice. I looked up at Bryan's face. He'd been my family's bodyguard for years, and now he'd been sent to be my assassin. "Nice eyes."

Chaos broke out.

Laurel and her humans turned on the vampires. Guns went off—guns that could hurt vampires but not kill them. Teeth ripped into flesh. It was bloody and terrible. Nathan and I were forgotten as each group tried to establish dominance and claim me as the prize. Free of Laurel, Nathan scurried through the fray and jerked me away toward the front door.

"Come on," he said. "We have to go while they're fighting."

We looked out the front window. Our car was still parked on the street, but it wasn't alone: Four vampires stood watch near it. Bryan wasn't stupid enough to leave us an easy escape.

"What do you think?" Nathan cast an uneasy glance outside.

"I think the two of us might be able to distract one of them."

"You took out two at the border."

"That was luck. I totally caught the one by surprise, and I just barely got in the car before I—"

I screamed as something sharp and biting tore into my leg. My knees buckled, and I sank to the floor before Nathan's arm could catch me. Glancing down, I saw blood on the thigh of my jeans. We both looked over and saw the old housekeeper standing with a gun.

"Mr. Arcangeli told me to make sure you didn't leave."

Mr. Arcangeli. Bryan. Laurel's housekeeper was on Bryan's payroll. That's how he'd been tipped off I was coming. She still had the gun pointed at us, but her hands were shaking. Nathan leapt at her, and she wasn't nearly fast enough to stop him. It was both sad and comical watching him wrestle the old woman, but the pain in my leg made it hard to feel too sorry for her. In the end, he was fairly gentle. Once he had the gun, he shoved her far away from us. Not surprisingly, she didn't make a play to get the gun back. Instead, she turned and ran shrieking into the other room, calling for Bryan.

Holding the gun in one hand, Nathan slid his other arm around me and helped me stand. "I'll be okay," I told him. "I should heal in fifteen minutes or so. Half-hour, tops."

"We don't have that kind of time. Come on."

"The car—"

"We can't get it. Let's just get out of here, and worry about transportation once we're away from this hellhole."

Half-dragging me, Nathan led us down a hall that went out to the kitchen. The kitchen connected to the living room—where the action appeared to be fading, much to my dismay. I felt pretty confident Bryan's group had won, but there must have been enough loose ends for them to not notice us in the kitchen yet. A small door led out to the backyard.

We stumbled outside, moving at an agonizingly slow pace. On the far side of the lot, we could see a stand of trees that hadn't been clear-cut yet. We aimed for those, hoping we could hide out.

"We can't stay too long," he warned. "The sun'll be up soon."

"Don't worry about me."

"Lucy . . . what are you going to do? About the prophecy?" Nathan's voice was both curious and awed. "I still can't believe it's real."

"Well, somebody does, or else all of that crap wouldn't be going on at the house." I sighed. "I don't know what I'm going to do. I don't want any of it. I don't want anyone to die. I'm scared of my eighteenth birthday. I would give anything to avoid that first kill . . . but at the cost of killing my own people? I don't want either race to dominate the other. I don't want more killing. I wish . . . I wish there could be a balance between us."

We came to a stop at the edge of the trees. Nathan's eyes were alive with excitement. We stood close, my breathing hard because of the extra exertion. "Maybe that's what you're supposed to do. Maybe you aren't supposed to destroy either race. You could bring them— bring us—together."

I shook my head. "I don't know. I don't know."

"I do."

Bryan materialized from the darkness. The housekeeper had apparently reported our escape.

He approached us slowly, smiling. It was still hard to believe this was the same Bryan I'd grown up around. I'd always trusted him, looked to him to defend us from other vampires. I'd watched him kill other vampires too—but I'd never expected to be one of them.

"I'm sorry, Lucy," he said. "I really am. But this is for the greater good. You've always been too squeamish about humans—we can't risk letting you have this power. I'm sorry."

"Stop." A voice cut through the night. Laurel approached from the side, trailed by one of her men. Both were armed, guns pointed at Bryan. She was gasping and bloody, and I couldn't believe she was still upright after what I'd witnessed in the living room. I wondered how many of her cohorts were still alive. She and the man behind her might be it.

"Unbelievable," said Bryan, echoing my thoughts.

He eyed my leg and turned toward the new threat, again neglecting us for a more urgent fight—a fight that I suspected was going to be very, very short from the looks of Laurel and her friend. Nathan touched my arm.

"Come on, while they're distracted. . . ."

"We can't outrun him. Even with a head start."

Bryan flew toward Laurel's counterpart. They fell to the ground, and though I couldn't quite see what was happening, I heard a shriek and wet, ripping noises. I pictured that happening to me and Nathan, imagined my own life—the life I'd wanted to do so many things with—vanishing. Snuffed out like a candle. Adrenaline burned through me, powering through the bullet's pain, and I took a deep breath. I turned toward Nathan.

"Did you mean it before?" I said quietly. The man had stopped screaming. "About doing something great? Doing something that will change the world?"

Those beautiful, beautiful eyes widened. He understood. He knew exactly what I meant, and that's when I got it. That's why I'd been drawn to him from the beginning—and vice versa. It's why despite every reason he had to hate me, he still couldn't leave me. The disc had said I'd know who I was meant to choose when I created my thirteen.

"You'll be able to kill them," I said. Laurel was screaming now. "But they can still kill you. And they'll try. They'll keep trying to kill both of us."

There was no hesitation, no fear. I thought about the determination I'd witnessed in him all night. Nathan had the capacity to do so many things—he just wanted the chance to prove it. "Do it. Whatever you have to."

I didn't hesitate either. In a flash, I rested my fingers on his head and murmured the words that had burned themselves into my mind when I'd seen the disc.

"By moon and dark, by sun and light, I bind you to me, now and forever, life to life, death to death." I felt something crackle through the air as I spoke.

My mouth moved to his neck, and I let my teeth sink into his skin. The scent that had haunted me all night, his skin and sweat, flooded my nose, just as his blood spilled into my mouth. It was salty and warm and the most wonderful thing I'd ever tasted. This was why vampires wanted humans. This was why we killed them.

But really, my bite was only a kiss. I pulled back, feeling that power continue to build between us. I had barely stepped away when Bryan came flying toward us, Laurel and the man dead. All vampires were dangerous, but Bryan was one of the most lethal. Few could stop him.

But Nathan did.

I'd never expected to see anyone match Bryan—certainly not a human. For Bryan, it must have been like hitting a brick wall. He staggered back, shocked. Nathan kept coming, beautiful and deadly. He punched Bryan in the face, causing the vampire to stumble again. Bryan came to his senses and pushed forward, taking the offensive.

For a moment, it was a deadlock. Neither could hit the other. Then, Nathan snaked in and grabbed Bryan by the shirt. Nathan slammed him into a tree and punched him—once, twice. Bryan's head hit the tree each time, and when the third blow came, he collapsed. We stared at each other, stunned.

"We have to go," I said. "The others will come. My leg's just about healed."

"Is he dead?"

"He will be soon, once the sun comes up. And so will I. We have to find a place to hide out for the night. Now."

When Nathan didn't move, I realized he was in shock, shock over what he had just done and what he could now do.

"Can you do it?" I asked, suddenly afraid for no reason I could explain. "Can you stay with me?"

I hate them. I really hate them. If I had the power to kill every vampire in the world and make things the way they used to be, I would.

Nathan had made his feelings about vampires clear all night. It was one thing to say, "Sure! Make me a vampire killer!" in the heat of battle—and another thing to accept what it meant afterward. *And who it had bound you to.* Slowly, he seemed to wake out of his daze. He turned toward me.

His hand reached out and rested on the side of my neck. His fingers were warm, yet sent chills through me. My whole body seemed to want his, yet at the same time, I realized what I'd done. I'd created a human who could kill vampires. A human who could kill *me*. And as his hand rested on the side of my neck, I realized that all powers being equal, he was built stronger than me. He could end this now, kill me, and go on a vampire killing spree. No discrimination. No thought for a better world.

Time stood still. Everything rested on him and his choice. The hand on my neck tightened ever so slightly, and then it slid up and cupped the side of my face. He kissed me, and as our lips touched, I felt all the power of that initial bite race back through us. I wrapped my arms around him, our bodies growing warm. I had never experienced anything like this. We broke apart, dizzy and restless.

"That was . . . wow," he said.

I swallowed. "I didn't know that was part of the prophecy."

"That wasn't prophecy," he said, still trailing fingers along my face. "That was us."

"I thought you hated vampires?"

"You don't treat me like vampires do. You don't even treat me like most humans do."

It was probably the highest compliment he could give. My heart fluttered. I wanted him to kiss me again, but dawn was closing in. "What are you going to do?" I had to be sure I could trust him with this power. "Will you stay with me?"

"I'm bound to you, remember?"

"Are you—"

"Bound, Lucy," he said firmly. "Life to life, death to death."

I didn't question him again. "Then let's go. The sun's going to come up."

"And the moon's going down," he murmured. "How long until the next blue one? Until your birthday?"

"Eight months."

"We'd better hurry then."

He caught hold of my hand, and together, we headed off into the night, off to change the world.

Free

A Story of Evernight

CLAUDIA GRAY

New Orleans
Summer 1841

The house on Royal Street was as refined as any other in New Orleans. Cast-iron scrollwork decorated the gate that enclosed the small garden, where a profusion of hydrangeas bloomed in crimson and violet. No loud parties ever took place within, and the oil lamps always dimmed at a reasonable hour. The honey-colored paint was in good taste, as were the modest, fashionable gowns worn by the ladies who lived there.

Yet it was not a respectable house.

"You mustn't pay those ladies any mind." Althea plaited Patrice's hair as she spoke, her fingers quick and sure. Althea was Patrice's mother, although Patrice was not allowed to call her "Mamma" when anyone else was around. Lately, Patrice had not bothered to call her that in private, either. "Just jealous, every last one of them. What wouldn't they give for a dress made of real Parisian satin? They're poor. You and I—we will never be poor."

"They didn't say we were poor. They said we—that we were bought and paid for."

Althea's hands closed around Patrice's shoulders. The fine cotton of her chemise wrinkled beneath Althea's grip. "We are free women of color," she said quietly. "We will never be slaves. Never."

Patrice had seen slaves working on the levee, without even hats or scarves to shield them from the punishing sun, sweat gleaming on their skin as overseers cursed them to work even harder. She had seen girls years younger than herself scrubbing front stoops on their hands and knees, knuckles ashy and raw from lye. She had seen scars around wrists and ankles, the red ugly welts that showed where shackles had once been. And she knew that cruelties like these took place in other refined houses in the French Quarter, in New Orleans, throughout the South. No, Patrice and Althea were more fortunate than any slaves.

But being a free woman of color did not mean being truly free. This was even more true for Patrice and her mother—who lived in luxury provided by wealthy white men in an "arrangement" that felt as unbreakable as any chain.

Once Patrice's hair had been braided into elaborate buns and loops, Althea treated her like some fragile glass trinket that might shatter before the ball. "Don't you even think about lying down and flattening your hair," Althea said as she loosely tied a lace scarf around Patrice's head. "You can sleep all day before tomorrow's dance if you're tired."

Patrice, who had made other plans during her mother's afternoon naps for months now, simply nodded.

After Althea had left her alone, Patrice watched the clock on the mantel. Mr. Broussard had brought it as a gift after his last trip to Europe—a gift for her, not for her mother. This attention had angered Althea, who had spoken sharply to Patrice for a week afterward. Patrice suspected that was why she was being presented this summer instead of the next, when she would be sixteen.

As if I would want such a monstrosity, Patrice thought as she looked at the bronze nymphs surrounding the clock face. The clock's creator had taken great pains to prominently display all the nymphs' uncovered breasts. *As if I would want any attention from Mr. Broussard.*

Of course, Althea and Patrice both knew that what Patrice wanted didn't matter.

Once twenty minutes had passed, Patrice rose and swiftly put on a simple calico housedress and a pair of slippers. The stairs creaked as she hurried downstairs, but Patrice didn't worry. Althea, like most free residents of New Orleans, was sound asleep. The June heat and humidity were so punishing that free people did not attempt to do anything at midday except nap. The whole city fell quiet, and it became very easy to avoid being seen.

Patrice tiptoed out the back door toward the shade provided by a magnolia tree's broad, shining leaves. She was still blinking, blinded by the sun, when two hands reached out from that darkness and grabbed her.

"Amos," she whispered, before his mouth closed over hers.

They sank to their knees together, wrapped in each other. Amos's embrace was tight, almost demanding, but after the first few eager kisses, he pulled back. They smiled at each other, giddy as always with their successful escapes.

"Lookin' fancy," he said. With one finger, he lifted the edge of her lace scarf to peek at the complicated hairdo beneath. "Wish I could see you tonight, when you dress up so fine."

"I wish too." Patrice leaned against his broad chest. Blacksmithing had made his muscles as thick as cordwood. He smelled like ashes and horses, like the earthy, dirty real world that she'd been sheltered from throughout her life.

She did not find the smell unpleasant. Amos's clothes carried the scent of his work. This reminded her that, despite his poverty, Amos was freer than she would ever be.

Amos's former master was widely considered to be a soft, foolish person by the finer residents of New Orleans—a subject of ridicule by the proper white ladies who would cross the street to avoid walking near women like Althea. This master had allowed Amos to train as a blacksmith, then hired him out to people at reasonable wages.

Many slave owners did this for various skilled trades. But Amos had been allowed to keep part of his wages. Amos was so skilled at his craft, so very much in demand, that within only a few years he had saved enough to buy his own freedom. And his master had let him! The gossips in town could devise no explanation for such eccentricity.

"This party tonight." Amos said abruptly. "They don't make up their minds right away, do they? It wouldn't happen as soon as that."

Patrice had hidden from this hard truth as long as she could. They had to face it now. "No, probably nobody will pay court to me tonight. But somebody will, Amos, before the season's over. What difference does it make, if it's tonight or two months from now?"

"Two months with you is worth a lot to me. Especially if it's the last two months we ever have." Wearily, Amos leaned back against the trunk of the magnolia tree. "If Althea would've waited one more year, I could've put enough money aside. Enough to get a couple rooms for us. We might have been husband and wife."

"I don't think she would ever have let me marry."

"Let you? *Let* you?" Amos was not angry, only disbelieving. "Your problem is you were never a slave. You don't know what it means, bein' free. If you did, you wouldn't abide her 'letting' you do a thing."

"Amos—"

"Why wouldn't Althea let you marry? Why wouldn't she want somethin' decent for you, instead of—"

He didn't say the rest aloud. That was his way of being kind.

"She wants grandchildren who will have even lighter skin than mine," Patrice said. "She wants to know that there will always be a wealthy white man's name to use if the patrollers stop me—so nobody can ever claim that I'm not free."

Probably Althea also wanted a source of support if Mr. Broussard ever tired of her, but Patrice never spoke of that. She didn't even like thinking about that possibility, because if Althea could someday be abandoned, Patrice could be too.

Amos sighed heavily, his anger exhausted. They always came back to this in the end—to resignation, regret, and yearning for everything they'd been denied. "I imagine it sometimes. You and me. How it might be for us."

"I do too."

In truth, Patrice had no idea whether she could be a good wife to Amos. To be a poor man's wife, she would have to cook and churn butter and scrub clothes on a washboard—chores she'd never had to learn how to do. Althea had never learned either. Slave girls belonging to Mr. Broussard came over each day to take care of such things. Sometimes the slaves' disdainful stares hurt more than those of the white ladies. They would look up from their work, hair hidden under kerchiefs, eyes narrowed, as if to say, *Who do you think you're fooling?*

How they would have laughed, if she had thrown her wealth away to marry Amos. But it would have been worth it, if she and Amos could only have had a chance.

She put her hands on either side of his face, and they kissed again. What began gently soon became more intense. Amos leaned her backward, into the soft carpet of fallen magnolia leaves, and his heavy body covered hers. His homespun shirt was open at the neck, and she could feel the warmth of his skin through her thin dress.

They had never become lovers, because Amos had old-fashioned ideas. Patrice, who could not afford to be old-fashioned, arched her body against his so that he would feel the swell of her breasts, the tautness of her belly.

"If only you were my wife," he whispered against her throat. "How I could love you."

"You could love me now, if you only would."

He pushed her aside, almost roughly, and his face twisted into a grimace. Then he looked at her, his eyes desperate. "Leave with me. Tonight, after the party."

"Amos!"

"We can do it." He clutched at the sleeve of her dress. "A blacksmith can find work anywhere. All we have to do is go."

"We don't have the money." This was no time for foolishness. "We don't know a soul outside New Orleans. If we ran away, we could never call on any of our white folks for help, not ever again. How long do you think we'd stay free? A month? A week?"

Amos's shoulders sagged. The truth had defeated him.

She put her hand upon the open V exposed at the neck of his shirt. "I don't want some white man to be the first to touch me."

"I don't want to do you shame."

"We love each other. There's less shame in that than—than anything else I'll ever have."

They were silent together for a while longer, and she watched Amos's face carefully. In his eyes were his love and desire for her, doing battle with his idea of what was respectable for them both. Patrice had never been respectable, not really, so she couldn't understand why it was so hard for him to choose. When she saw the slight relaxing of the tension in his broad shoulders, she felt she had won.

Patrice whispered, "My room is in the back of the house. The small balcony—you know the one?" Amos nodded. "I'll leave the shutters unlatched. We should be home no later than midnight. Come—maybe an hour later than that. You'll be all right if you have your papers; people know you. All right?"

She still thought he might refuse, out of misguided devotion to her. But he said, "I'll come to you."

❧☙

Amos departed before the sun had left its zenith. Patrice went inside and took a hasty sponge bath, so that her mother would not smell horses and ashes on her skin. By the time Althea had awakened, Patrice sat demurely on the chaise in the parlor, wearing her silk wrapper and reading Coleridge's *Ballads*.

"You seem to have perked up," Althea said. "About time you realized how lucky you are."

Patrice, half-crazy with anticipation, hid her smile behind her mouth.

As the afternoon cooled and the shadows grew long, they began to prepare for the first quadroon ball of the season. Tonight the young ladies would meet the wealthy scions who wanted a black wife to tide them over until they could take a white one.

Time for a girl to look her best, she thought bitterly.

Patrice dabbed Florida water on her wrists and at her throat, and she tucked verbena sachets into the folds of her gown so that she would smell sweet no matter how warm the crowded room became. Powder would keep her face from becoming shiny and make her skin look even paler.

Althea tied a bit of lace around Patrice's throat and fastened a cameo in front. Then she laced Patrice into her corset; once it was so tight that Patrice felt almost dizzy, Althea proclaimed that she would now fit into her gown.

"Eighteen inches," Althea said proudly as she helped Patrice step into her hoop skirt. "That's as thin as my waist, before I had you."

Struggling for breath, Patrice did not care about any of that—at least, not until she saw herself in the mirror.

The satin of her dress was the palest lilac, and fine lace ruffled at the sleeves and upon the broad, bell-shaped skirt. Her bodice was low enough to show off the new curves of her bosom. Patrice knew there was no girl in New Orleans who could outshine her that night, and for a moment her pride eclipsed her shame.

I wish Amos could see me like this. He'd be amazed.

But he wouldn't see her tonight. Instead, she would be on display to the men who sought to take her as a concubine—including, probably, the one who would take her away from Amos forever.

The thrill of anticipation she felt for tonight, for Amos, could not entirely eclipse the knowledge of her ultimate fate. She and Amos would become lovers soon, but her destiny was still to be a white man's mistress. His plaything. His possession in all but name.

"Pull tighter!" Althea grunted, bringing Patrice back to the here and now, in which she was lacing up her mother's corset in turn. "I swear, I don't know where your mind wanders off to sometimes."

℘◌℘

The carriage called for them just after nightfall. Patrice and Althea rode through the streets to the Salle de Lafayette. Horses' hooves and wagon wheels rattled against the cobblestone streets, and the gaslights on each corner kept the dark at bay.

They swept inside the ballroom side by side, but that was the last moment Patrice would spend with her mother all night. As usual, Althea's friends drew her into a corner for punch and gossip. Patrice might have sought her own friends, who were at least as nervous as she was, but she wasn't in the mood for company.

The band tuned up its instruments as the men began to enter. At first, the arrivals were mostly the older gentlemen, the ones Patrice already knew—the men who kept company with their mothers. She saw Mr. Broussard staring at her with ill-concealed interest, at least until Althea took his arm and began paying him the sweet compliments he liked so much.

Patrice also glimpsed a tall man with white hair—Laurence Deveraux, whose last name she and her mother kept although he had last visited Althea many years ago. His face reminded Patrice of her own. Although no one had ever dared to call him her father, Patrice knew the truth.

Really, she did not expect Mr. Deveraux to pay attention to her. He never had before. But it would have been nice for him to at least glance her way and see how pretty she looked in her satin dress.

Then the younger men came. One carriage after another emptied out on the walk below, each one filled with boisterous, laughing gentlemen, most of them fresh from university. They strode into the club proudly, their cravats bright against white shirts with high collars. They wore broad smiles and waistcoats of watered silk, and their laughter was too knowing for Patrice's taste.

One of them did not laugh.

He caught Patrice's attention right away. It was only because he was quieter than the others in the room, but he was handsome too. He seemed to be a few years older than some of the other boys, and he held himself with dignity. His chestnut hair was as long as a girl's.

His dark eyes swept through the room, bored and disdainful, as though he hardly expected to see anything that would interest him. Yet when his gaze arrived at her, he paused.

Patrice ought to have behaved like a proper lady, averting her eyes while unfolding her fan. Instead, she lifted her chin and stared back.

I won't play the demure little girl, she swore. *Not for him or for anyone! If I let him see how much I hate him, then he won't court me. I'll have longer to spend with Amos.*

Slowly, he smiled.

Surely he had to be smiling at someone else. Patrice turned her head and started to push through the crowd toward the window. It would be easy enough to lose him in the crush.

Then a hand closed over her shoulder.

She turned to see the man with chestnut hair, who had crossed the busy room with surprising speed. The white kid leather of his glove was soft against her bare skin. "There you are," he said, as though they were old friends, long separated by chance.

Patrice pulled away. "Sir, we have not been introduced."

"I am Julien Larroux."

At first she didn't know how to respond. Unmarried girls and young gentlemen did not introduce themselves to each other; they waited to be introduced by a mutual friend or a chaperon. Julien had been rude to approach her like this, but it seemed ruder to walk away after he had given her his name. "Patrice Deveraux."

"A delight to meet you." Julien's bottle-green eyes focused on her with disconcerting intensity. "Tell me, Miss Deveraux, is this your first dance?"

"Yes, sir, it is." She ought to have fawned on about how elegant the arrangements were, but Patrice did not want to charm this man. If he desired her, then he was a threat; for the first time, she might be looking into the eyes of the man who would take her from Amos for good.

Her brusque answer seemed to please him. His lips were dark against his alabaster skin; Patrice found the contrast surprisingly sensual—yet not nearly as handsome as Amos's burnished dark features. "You do not flirt like the other girls."

"You flirt just like the other boys. Though less politely, I should say." *There, that will get rid of him.*

Instead, Julien laughed softly. "You don't want to be here, do you?"

"Don't presume to know what I want."

"You have pride. Something most of the women here are sorely lacking. Many of the men too. They crawl. They conform. You—you hold your head high. I believe you have spirit, Miss Deveraux."

Patrice wished she could have slapped him. "If you can't behave properly, I'll have to fetch my chaperon."

"In your heart, I think you don't care very much about proper behavior." Julien's pale eyes seemed to be staring down into her soul, glimpsing her plan to welcome Amos to her bed. Patrice felt the almost irresistible urge to run away from him, as though he were a thief on a darkened road late at night instead of a a gentleman at a party. But fear and confusion kept her frozen in place. He continued, "I shall behave properly—for now. May I have the very great honor of the first dance?"

She could think of no valid excuse to refuse. "You may, sir."

The first dance was the Virginia Reel, a bouncy dance that made everyone laugh and clap their hands. Usually Patrice enjoyed dancing a reel. With so many couples upon the dance floor—three dozen, at least—she should have had more fun than ever.

Not with Julien Larroux.

She told herself that he unnerved her merely because she could not immediately understand him. These other proud, boastful boys—she did not have to meet them to know them. They had no concerns any deeper than the shiny pomade in their hair. Julien danced as well as any of them, never missing a step, and he smiled all the while. But it was not the silly grin the other men wore; it was cool, almost mocking. Worst of all, he seemed to think that Patrice should be in on the joke.

The dance ended, and for a while she escaped to other partners—which was not much escape at all, given their frank appraisal of her charms. But halfway through the night, Julien reclaimed her for a waltz.

"A far superior dance, the waltz." Julien's hand rested upon her back as he led her through the movements. He had thin, bony fingers that made her think of claws. The air was thick with the scent of camellias. "Much more intimate."

"I quite agree."

"Did your mother tell you that?" His eyebrow arched disdainfully. "To agree with anything I say?"

"She did say that, actually. Not that I pay her any mind. I said I agreed with you because I really do. As you should know by now, if you say something foolish, I'll tell you so."

His smile broadened. Julien's teeth were almost unnaturally white. "You don't act like a young lady who's trying to catch a man."

"Perhaps I'm not." She thought of Amos and the way he had kissed her beneath the magnolia tree.

"Why else are you here?"

"I have no other choice," Patrice said flatly.

Such honesty ought to have wiped the smirk from Julien's face. It did not. "You may have more choices than you think."

"I suppose you're referring to yourself?"

"In a manner of speaking."

So soon! Patrice had hoped to have another few months at home before she would have to give herself to some stranger. Yet here was Julien Larroux as much as asking for her already.

"Why me?" she whispered.

"Why not one of your vapid friends?" He nodded toward the corner, where an awkward young girl was valiantly attempting to flirt with chubby Beauregard Wilkins. "Because you wear your satin and lace the way knights once wore armor. I think you see life as a battle—and I like a fighter."

Patrice knew she ought to have been grateful that at least the man who sought her was someone of intelligence and discernment. That, or she should have been terrified of the inner sense she had that something about Julien Larroux was simply *wrong*.

But all she could think was: *He's taking me away from Amos. Taking me soon.*

After the party, during the carriage ride home, Althea was beside herself with glee. "They say that Mr. Larroux is new to the city, but clearly he's of good family, and tremendously rich. He's taken a whole suite in the finest hotel, and he's been asking about a mansion on St. Charles Avenue."

Patrice shrugged. "Has he spoken to Mr. Broussard?"

"Not yet, but I expect he'll pay a call in the morning."

"How can you be so happy?" Patrice whispered. "How can you want this for me?"

The cool, artificial smile never left Althea's lips. "This is all you could ever have," she said. "What else could I want?"

Her implication, clearly, was, *What else could you want?*

Julien Larroux was genteel and handsome. His wealth would buy her a well-appointed house, not unlike the one she'd grown up in, and countless beautiful dresses and bonnets. His slaves would clean her home. She might even have her own horse and carriage.

Those were the sort of prizes that Althea valued. Patrice wanted something else: freedom to make her own choices. As of tonight, any chance of that had been stolen from her forever.

At least I'll be with Amos tonight, she told herself. *They'll never be able to take that away from me.*

As they descended from the carriage, Patrice lifted her skirts to avoid the mud. In the corner of her eye, she caught a bit of movement at the fence beside the house.

Her pulse quickened.

❧◯❧

That night, she lay in bed, tremulous with excitement and fear. Her thin cotton nightgown stuck to her sweaty body; the New Orleans heat did not relent, even after midnight.

We'll have to be very quiet, she thought.

Judging from the noises she'd sometimes heard from her mother's room during Mr. Broussard's visits, quiet didn't come easily at such times. But Patrice felt she could acquit herself better than Althea.

Then she thought of Amos's broad, callused hands upon her—without even her nightgown between them—and realized remaining silent might be a challenge.

Patrice sucked on the corner of her sheet, a nervous habit from childhood that she still slipped into from time to time. She did not want to admit that she was nervous, that she could ever be frightened of Amos. Yet her heart raced, beating so hard that her breasts trembled with every thump. Her breathing was fast and shallow.

The shutters over her windows showed thin stripes of moonlight. She watched them, eyes wide, waiting for some shadow or movement.

A sharp squeal outside made her jump, but Patrice almost instantly realized it came from the side gate. No doubt the stray cats were fighting again.

She wondered if Julien Larroux would allow her to keep a cat.

Within a few weeks, Patrice would live in a stranger's house. He would want to touch her, and she would not have the right to say no. She'd grown up knowing that this would be her fate; once, she'd believed that if the man in question were only young and handsome, all her dreams would come true. How empty those dreams seemed now.

Downstairs, on the back porch, a board creaked.

Amos, she thought. And yet Patrice did not feel her heart leap with gladness. Instead, she clutched her sheet. Her ears pricked, almost painfully, in search of another sound.

It had to be Amos coming to see her. This was what they had planned, the time she had told him. Who else could it be?

Yet Althea had always warned her to keep the shutter doors latched. Otherwise, anyone could get in. Absolutely anyone.

It's Amos. Don't be silly.

The side beam of the porch groaned with new weight, and then she heard the unmistakable sound of someone taking hold of the iron scrollwork that bordered her balcony.

Latch the shutters, Patrice thought. *Wait until Amos says his name. He can whisper without being heard, and you'll be right there. It's him—it has to be him—but just in case—*

At the last possible moment, she leaped out of bed and ran on shaky legs toward the window. The thin slits of moonlight through the shutters suddenly broke into a shadow shaped like a man. Footsteps on the balcony accompanied the shadow getting bigger, getting closer. Patrice reached for the latch—she still had time—

Her longing for Amos overcame her, and she hesitated for only an instant.

The shutters flew open. There stood Julien Larroux.

Patrice sucked in a breath to scream, but his pale hand shot out to clasp her mouth. "Silence," he murmured. He no longer wore the charming smile he'd used at the ball. His grin now looked more like the bared teeth of a feral beast.

She jerked her head to the side. "You get out," Patrice whispered. Her voice trembled. "Get out this instant or I'll scream."

"Scream?" Julien's angular face lit up, as though she'd suggested a delightful surprise. "Yes, scream for your mother. When she comes in, I'll explain how you left the shutters unlatched for me. How else could I have entered your bedroom? What an—*obliging* girl you are, to have helped me."

"I'll take a caning if it means getting rid of you."

His bottle-green eyes blazed. "When I called you a fighter, I spoke the truth."

"You'll get a fight if you don't leave." Patrice balled her hands into fists. She took some comfort from the fact that Amos would arrive any moment now, and when he saw what Julien was trying to do—

Amos would fight him. He might try to kill Julien Larroux—a white man. And for that, Amos would be hung, either by the law or a lynch mob.

Patrice whispered, "What do I have to do before you'll go away?"

"How unromantic you make it sound."

"Can we just get it over with?" She might have to endure Julien Larroux's touch, but she'd be damned if she'd pretend to enjoy it.

Julien tilted his head, considering. "Only one very simple thing, my fierce Patrice. Allow me to kiss your neck."

". . . what?"

"One kiss upon your throat." Julien's long, pale fingers stroked the line of her jaw, then dipped lower until they rested upon a vein. His eyes darkened, and Patrice knew he was reveling in her quickened pulse. "Allow me that—with no struggle, no cry—and afterward, I shall leave. You and I will not be alone together again until you desire it."

That will be never. Although Patrice doubted this evening's transaction would be so simple or painless, she could not refuse while Amos was at risk.

"Very well." Patrice took a small step forward. "Go ahead."

Julien smiled at her. "Tilt your head backward—yes, like that—and pull at the neck of your nightgown."

Patrice trembled so violently that she thought she might fall, but she shook from suppressed rage as much as fear. Her fingers fumbled at the neck of her gown as she tugged it down, exposing her throat.

Then Julien clasped her shoulders and pulled her close. He smelled—strange, not exactly unfamiliar, but not like anyone else she had ever met. Something metallic had seeped into the air, and the odor reminded her of—of—

Of a butcher shop, her mind supplied.

Patrice's eyes opened wide. Her soul understood something her brain could not yet comprehend. In that instant, she would have screamed—but Julien's teeth sank into her throat.

Then there was only darkness, and pain, yet something sweet within the pain.

§✄ Q

Patrice awakened to a scream.

At first, as she pushed herself upright in bed, she thought she must have dreamed the sound. Hadn't she just been having a nightmare? None of the details were clear; like most dreams, they were dissolving in the bright light of day.

Blinking at the brilliant sunshine that flooded through the glass doors to her balcony, Patrice thought that Althea had kept her promise and let her sleep awfully late that day. Yet she still felt exhausted, almost weak. She hoped she wasn't getting sick. This was the time of year when yellow fever often struck.

Patrice frowned. The glass doors were unlatched. Didn't she always remember to latch them?

(*Amos's eyes, soft in the night, shining with love for her. "I'll come to you."*)

Yet he had not come.

Her confusion grew. Surely, if Amos had not come to her, she would have stayed up all night fretting about it, or worrying that he'd been caught out after curfew. Yet she lay in her bed, all tucked in. The only thing out of the ordinary was the open neck of her nightgown.

It seemed as if she were forgetting something—something important. But what?

My mind is clouded, Patrice thought. *Maybe I'm taking sick after all.*

Then she heard the scream again, and this time she knew it was real.

"Mamma?" she cried, as she grabbed her silk wrapper. Her feet, swollen from dancing the night before, jolted with pain on every step. Slipping into her wrapper as she headed downstairs, she corrected herself. "Althea?"

Patrice flung open the side door and saw that a small group had gathered around the side gate. Althea leaned against a lamp post, half in a swoon, while a small child fanned her with his hand.

"What's happening? Is Althea sick?" Patrice hurried closer, but even as she did so she realized the crowd was not paying attention to her mother, but to something outside the side gate.

Mr. Ebbets, who owned the next house, said heavily, "Child, this is nothing for you to see. Someone has been killed by dogs."

"Dogs?" It seemed too shocking to believe. Or was there some other reason she didn't believe it? Patrice felt herself flashing back to her nightmare—not images or sounds, because she could not remember, and yet there was some kind of connection.

"We've sent for the police," Mr. Ebbets said. "Get your mother inside. Ladies shouldn't be exposed to such as this. That poor boy's throat had been ripped out. Had to be dogs, or some other kind of wild animal."

Patrice slowly said, "But who—the man who died—"

"The blacksmith. That free boy from the Marigny. Didn't he shoe your horse last winter?"

On the ground, amid the feet of curious gawkers, lay a long, well-muscled arm as thick and dark as cordwood.

∞∞

By the afternoon, the police had taken away what was left of Amos. Althea acted as though nothing had happened.

"You've cried all day," she said crossly, snatching the coverlet off the bed so that Patrice lay uncovered. "Your eyes will bulge as big as a cow's."

"I don't care."

"What are you carrying on for? It's not as if that blacksmith was anyone to us." Althea paused at the foot of the bed. Her looped braids framed her narrow face, the style too girlish for her years. "Was he, Patrice?"

"No," Patrice said, because the time for telling Althea the truth was long past.

Althea took Patrice's pale yellow dress from the closet. "Let me do your hair, and we'll get you dressed. I suppose we'll be late for tonight's dance, but it can't be helped."

Patrice squeezed her eyes tightly shut, willing herself to be somewhere else, or someone else. She rubbed at her neck, where one spot was incredibly tender. Was she imagining that pain, because of what had been done to Amos's throat last night? "The shock—it's too much, Althea. Couldn't I stay home tonight?"

"And run the risk of Julien Larroux setting his cap for another girl? You're crazy. Get out of that bed."

Julien Larroux. Patrice's eyes flew open as memory returned.

(*His teeth in her neck, the metallic smell of blood, the sickening slurp as he swallowed, Patrice struggling against him all the while, unable to fight—*)

She put her hand to her throat again. The skin beneath her fingers felt raw, as though she'd splashed herself with the laundry lye.

Old women told stories about such creatures. Patrice had never listened to those stories—it was just more silliness and superstition, like Marie Laveau's tales about voodoo. Or so she'd always believed.

(*"That poor boy's throat had been ripped out. Had to be dogs, or some other kind of wild animal."*)

Patrice pushed herself upright in the bed.

"That's more like it," Althea said briskly, as she set hairpins out on the vanity table. "I see I only had to mention your beau to get you going."

"Yes," Patrice murmured. "I think I need to see Julien Larroux again."

❧

They arrived with the ball already in full swing, pushing into a room already full of laughing young people and the sounds of fiddlers playing. The candles on the walls had half-burned down, leaving ripples of melted tallow on the catch-plates below. Patrice still felt weak, and every sensation was too intense: the body heat of the party's crush, the scratchy lace around her throat, and the scent of the camellias pinned in her hair.

As Althea waved to Mr. Broussard, Patrice stepped away from her. At that moment, Julien's eyes met hers.

He looked even more unearthly than he had the night before. His bottle-green eyes flashed with excitement at the sight of her, and his long chestnut hair hung free past his shoulders. Julien gave her a dark-lipped smile.

By all rules of propriety, Patrice ought to have waited for him to come to her. Instead, she weeded her way through the party, on the outskirts of the whirling dancers, to find Julien first.

"You look lovely tonight," Julien said. He seemed to be enjoying some private joke. "It doesn't seem as if it's been a whole day since

I've seen you. Maybe you've been in my thoughts so much we might as well have been together all night."

"I want to talk to you," Patrice said. "Alone."

Sometimes, when the candlelight caught them just so, Julien's eyes seemed to have no color at all. "Shall we take some fresh air?"

They stepped outside. Clouds covered the moon that night, so the only illumination came from the windows of the Salle de Lafayette, where the dancers were silhouetted. One of the chaperons stepped forward as if to warn them back inside, but Julien gave him a piercing look that seemed to make the old man forget all about the young couple stealing into the back garden alone at night.

"Here we are, my dear Patrice." Julien laid his hands on her bare shoulders, just above the lacy sleeves of her dress. "Did you miss me too?"

Patrice said, "I think you came to my house last night. I think you killed Am—the blacksmith. I think you tried to kill me too."

"An interesting set of assertions." Julien's thumb made little circles against her skin. She felt a strange pull toward him, as though they were tied together in a way that left her unable to run. His lips were very near her hair. "Why would I want to do any of those things? Besides coming to your house at night, of course. Any man would want to be near you."

"I remember you being there. I remember that you bit me."

She whirled to face him, eager to see him caught off-guard. Instead, Julien smiled, and for once his delight appeared to be genuine. "Extraordinary! Most people can't remember it, unless they're kept awake, and I tucked you in safe and sound. And, if you were curious, quite as much a maid as I found you. Though I was tempted."

"Then it's true." Patrice covered the tender spot at her throat with her fingers. "You're—you're a vampire."

"And I want you to become one too."

Patrice tried to think of a reply to this, but could not. Words and imagination had both failed her. More than anything else, she wanted to run, but she remembered what Althea had told her that time they saw a mad dog on the street with foam flecking his jaws: *Don't run. If you run, that just gives him a reason to chase you.*

She closed her hands around the branch of a nearby tree, as if to steady herself—then quickly snapped off a length of wood, perhaps six inches. "I've heard stories about your kind. I know what to do." With that, Patrice brandished her new stake.

He merely laughed. "You've heard stories. Not the truth. For instance, stakes don't kill us."

Was he lying to save himself? No, Patrice realized. Julien remained completely unafraid of her. She felt small and foolish, and slowly she let the hand with the stake drop to her side.

"Fire, now—fire is dangerous. Beheading too." His silky chestnut hair streamed behind him, caught by a sudden breeze. "I tell you these things because you'll need to know them to be by my side. And also because you have no fire and no blade."

"Oh, God," Patrice whispered. She had always thought she had no choices in life, but she hadn't truly known what it meant to be trapped, not before this instant when she was caught in a vampire's thirsty gaze.

Julien took her hands in his. "I knew the moment I saw you that you had the spark. The strength. Our world is not for the weak, Patrice. Besides, this shallow, empty life of disguised servitude—you hate it. That hatred burns inside you like a bonfire. I want to give you power like you've never imagined. Together, we could make the world our feast."

Power.

In an instant, she knew she had one choice left. She intended to make it.

Patrice tilted her head back. "Drink."

"My beautiful girl." Julien's grin changed as his canine teeth shifted slowly into fangs. Despite a terrible shiver of fear, Patrice did not flee. It occurred to her that if the legends about vampires were true, she was about to die. If Amos had been alive, she could never have surrendered her life so easily. Without him, her path was clearer.

She glanced upward at the moon, silvery and shrouded with thin clouds. It was strange to think that this was the last thing she would ever see in her life. The moon had never looked so beautiful before.

Then Julien pushed her against the nearby tree, with his hands clamped around her arms like irons, and tore open her throat.

Pain eclipsed everything else, even Julien, even the moon.

so ca

Silence.

Patrice had never known that quiet could be so overpowering. She had never realized that she could hear her own heart beating, or that all the sounds she normally heard were filtered through the soft rush of blood in her eardrums. Now that was gone.

Her eyes fluttered open. She lay upon the ground, her pale yellow gown stained with mud. Julien stood above her, watching avidly.

I'm dead, she thought. Something vital in her—something strong, something good—was gone, and she felt hollowed-out. As though every sound she would ever hear from now on would only be an echo, as if everything she touched would be only an imitation of reality. The pure river of constant change that ran through every living being had been stilled in her, forever.

It did not hurt. Even the pain of dying had been better than being dead.

"You won't miss it for long," Julien said. "Not when you see what we can do."

Patrice slowly sat upright. Petals from the crushed camellia she'd been wearing fluttered down onto her dress. She could only think of one thing to say: "I'm hungry."

Julien grinned. "We all awaken hungry. Let's find you a snack, shall we? Ah, look, there's someone now."

Into the garden staggered Beauregard Wilkins, obviously quite drunk. For the first time Patrice realized that she could hear no music or hubbub from the party within; she must have been dead for at least a few hours.

Althea will be wondering where I am.

Beauregard clutched his ample belly, obviously in danger of losing control of himself, but he seemed to forget his own distress when he saw Julien standing above Patrice. "What's this?" he said. "Larroux, old boy, no need to be rough with the ladies."

"You needn't worry about Patrice," Julien said. "She's better than she's ever been. Aren't you, my darling?"

Patrice cocked her head. Somehow, she could hear Beauregard's heart beating. Every single thump was like a drumbeat summoning her. Within Beauregard, blood flowed—hot, living blood—

She pounced at him with strength she had never before possessed. He fell back beneath her, staring at her in horror as her fangs slid forth for the first time. It hurt, and yet it made her shiver with pleasure. It felt right.

This is what I am now.

Then she bit him, tearing into warm flesh to get at what she needed: blood. It flowed into her mouth, rich and hot and good, and Patrice swallowed eagerly, desperate for the taste of life again. Beauregard struggled for only a moment before he sagged to the ground, unconscious.

"That's good," Julien said. "My savage little Patrice."

When she could drink no more, Patrice sat up. Blood was sticky on her lips. Beauregard still breathed, which surprised her until she realized it shouldn't. "He'll forget he was bitten." Her own voice sounded strange to her now. "Just like I forgot."

"Undoubtedly Mr. Wilkins will awaken tomorrow in the belief that he passed out drunk, as he no doubt would have had you not come along. The scars from your bite will have all but faded by then. No evidence left behind. It all works very well, you see."

"It doesn't kill, then. Our drinking." How strange, to say "our" and mean vampires.

"Not unless we want it to, the way I wanted it to for you."

Julien helped her to her feet and offered her a handkerchief. She dabbed at her lips, staining the white linen red.

"What happens now?" she whispered.

"Now, my dear, we turn New Orleans into our playground. We could live together openly, if you choose. Shock the populace. Or there are other places we can go—places where no living creature could find us. I have so much to show you. So much for you to learn." His fingers traced along the low neckline of her dress, leaving no doubt as to what he wanted her to learn first.

When he offered her his arm, she took it. Her legs were unsteady—not from weakness but from the unexpected power flowing through her.

"Let's walk out the front door," Patrice said. "It's not as if the slaves will dare to say a word."

Julien smiled a slow, hot smile. "Excellent idea."

They walked back into the Salle de Lafayette, which by now was nearly deserted. A few flower petals from ladies' nosegays littered the floor, and half the candles had burned out. An elderly slave woman, her back bent with age and care, tottered around, blowing out the rest. A bucket and rags in the corner testified to the scrubbing she would have to begin soon. It had to be nearly dawn. One lone oil lantern flickered near the front door.

"Where do you want to go next?" Julien said.

"My mother's house."

"You weren't that fond of her, were you? I suppose she's about to get a lesson she'll never forget. I can't wait to see it for myself."

As he opened the door and strode onto the front stoop, Patrice paused in the doorway. "You won't be coming home with me."

"What do you mean?"

She grabbed the oil lantern and threw it at his face.

The glass lantern shattered, mingling the fire with the flammable oil that had splashed all over Julien's body. He screamed—a terrible, animal sound. His entire body was a mass of flame as he staggered backward, then fell onto the walk.

As firelight flickered upon Patrice's face, she thought of Amos and how long and hard he'd worked to be free. She thought of the good strong arms that had held her, and how Julien had left Amos crumpled in the alley like garbage. She thought of their last kiss.

The old slave woman appeared behind Patrice. When she saw Julien burning, she didn't shout for anyone to come help. She simply watched by Patrice's side.

Once it was over, and the charred thing on the walk would clearly never move again, Patrice said, "I'm Patrice Deveraux. If they need proof it was an accident, you can tell them I saw the whole thing."

"Drunk as those young bucks get, nobody will doubt it."

The two women shared a glance, and then Patrice began the long journey back home.

In her crumpled, muddy dress, Patrice suspected she made quite a sight. Fortunately, the streets were all but empty. Althea would be furious when Patrice got home, thinking that she had been giving Julien Larroux favors that he ought to have paid for. Patrice did not intend to put up with that kind of talk for long. She thought she would finish out the season by pretending to be human, drinking when she wished, learning about her powers. And how lovely she would look in silk and satin, her hair fixed just so. Julien had called her beauty her armor, and she intended never to be without her armor again. When you were beautiful, you could charm the people around you so that they never saw the darker truth.

After a few months, Patrice would know how to handle her new abilities. Then she could set out on her own.

"You there! Girl!"

Patrice stopped walking and turned. A group of lanky white men strolled toward her, half-incredulous, half-gleeful. They wore shabby overalls and tattered straw hats. She realized they were the patrollers who kept black people from walking around after curfew—the ones who assumed that anyone who wasn't white was a slave. "Can I help you?" she said coolly.

"You don't dress like a colored girl," the leader said with a snide smile. "You one of them Creole mistresses?" The others snickered lasciviously.

"I'm going home."

"You better answer my questions, gal. Are you slave or free?"

For the first time, Patrice realized she would never have to carry her papers with her again. If anyone challenged her—white or black, living or dead—she had the strength to tear out their throats.

She thought she might even enjoy it.

Patrice smiled. "I'm free."

About the Authors

P. C. Cast is the *New York Times* bestselling author of the young adult House of Night series, which she coauthors with her daughter. She also writes the popular Goddess Summoning Series for Berkley, as well as the Partholon fantasy series for LUNA. She lives and teaches in Oklahoma. You can check her out at www.pccast.net or www.houseofnightseries.com

❧❧❧

Cynthia Leitich Smith is the acclaimed YA author of *Tantalize* (2007) and its companions, *Eternal* (2009) and *Blessed* (forthcoming), all Gothic fantasies from Candlewick Press. She also has written several YA short stories as well as books for younger readers. *Tantalize* was a March 2007 Borders Original Voices selection, honored at the 2007 National Book Festival, and *The Horn Book* called it "an intoxicating romantic thriller." A graphic novel adaptation of *Tantalize* is in the works. Cynthia may be found on the Web at www.cynthialeitichsmith.com. She makes her home in Austin, Texas, with her husband, author Greg Leitich Smith.

❧❧❧

New York Times bestselling author **Kristin Cast** is only going to college because she loves education and lives to attend lectures. Okay, not really. Miss Cast currently attends the University of Tulsa and is a communications major. She has won awards for her poetry, as well as served as journalist for her high school newspaper, *Tiger Tales*, and as editor for her high school magazine, *Tiger Eye*. Miss Cast would like to become so famous people make fountains and/or shrines in her image. You can reach her through www.pccast.net.

❧❧❧

Rachel Caine is the author of more than twenty-five novels, most notably her bestselling Morganville Vampires series and Weather Warden series, as well as being a frequent contributor to BenBella Books's fiction and nonfiction projects. She writes constantly, and frequently gets paid for it, which always surprises and delights her. Visit her Web site at www.rachelcaine.com, and friend her on Livejournal, Facebook, and MySpace!

❧❧❧

Tanith Lee was born in 1947 in the UK. She worked in many jobs until becoming a full-time professional writer in 1975. She has to date written nearly 100 books and more than 260 short stories, four radio plays, and episodes of the cult TV series *Blake's 7*. She has won, or been shortlisted for, numerous awards. She lives in England with her husband, writer and artist John Kaiine, and two permanently hungry Tuxedo cats.

❧❧❧

Nancy Holder is the *USA Today* bestselling author of more than eighty novels and 200 short stories, essays, and articles. She is currently working with co-author Debbie Viguie on *Wicked: Resurrection* for Simon and Schuster. The author of *Pretty Little Devils*, she has contracted with Razorbill for two more YA horror novels. Contact her at www.nancyholder.com.

✥

Richelle Mead is the *New York Times* bestselling author of *Vampire Academy* and *Frostbite*. The third book in the series, *Shadow Kiss*, will be released in November 2008. A former middle school teacher, Richelle now writes full-time in Seattle. She buys far too many dresses, hasn't seen the surface of her desk in more than a year, and rarely gets up before noon. More information can be found at www.richellemead.com.

✥

Claudia Gray is the pseudonym of New York–based writer Amy Vincent. She is the author of the Evernight series of vampire novels set in the present day, in which Patrice is a character—now as a 160-year-old vampire. The first book, *Evernight*, came out in May 2008, and the second book in the series, *Stargazer*, will be released in March 2009.

ONLINE

Your Link to Teen Lit

Previews of upcoming Teen Libris titles,
plus tons more great teen lit content:
contests, interviews, book excerpts,
and more!

www.TeenLibris.com